TRANSITIONS:

Through Tumultuous Events…
A Man Will Rise

Written By
Demetrius D. Jackson

Shadow World
Productions

D1608045

Shadow World Productions
https://www.facebook.com/ShadowWorldProductions3/
https://www.instagram.com/shadowworldproductions3/

This book is a work of fiction. Names, characters, places or incidents are products of the author's imagination and are used fictitiously. Any resemblance to actual events or persons, living or dead, is entirely coincidental.

Transitions
Through Tumultuous Events... A Man Will Rise

First Edition Published 2005
Current Edition Published 2019

ISBN 0-9771133-0-2 (First Edition)
ISBN 9781797869322 (Current Edition)

Editor: Tarrance C. Jackson
Logo Designer: Justin Bryant

Dedicated to my parents, Denise Jackson and Elwin (Robby) Robinson. You've always believed in me.

Acknowledgements:

First and foremost, I would like to thank the Lord for blessing me with a tremendous gift. I would like to thank my mother, Denise Jackson, for all the inspiration you have given me without even saying a word. Your determination to achieve your goals has given me the determination to achieve mine. Robby, you have always been there for me since I can remember. You've taught me so much about being a man and how to navigate through this cruel world. Dennis, my brother, I would have never starting writing poetry if it weren't for you. You constantly challenged me to get better and I feel your belief in me has had a tremendous affect on my success as a poet. Thank you!

Tarrance, my wife, you have blessed me with two wonderful children, and you continue to propel me forward. You are my biggest fan and my greatest critic. The heights I achieve are a result of you having my back.

Thank you to all of my friends who constantly encouraged me to write a book. Believe me, I was listening all of that time, I just needed to handle some other business first. Another thank you goes to all of my friends who have been true friends from day one. You've been there when times were rough and when times were going great.

To my bruhs of Phi Beta Sigma G.O.M.A.B. and to my sorors of Zeta Phi Beta much love. Let's keep the blue and white family ties strong.

CHILDHOOD

INTRO

Went through my trials and tribulations now at the moment that I've dreamt
A recollection of my life where has all the time went?
Many moments well spent and still the struggle to persevere
As I was inventing what you see I was something you couldn't hear
Now I'm gonna run you through this journey and events that made Marcellous
At the cunning and conniving and near death from others jealous
It's a struggle to even tell this, but I'll do the best I can
Close your eyes and visualize as I lead you by the hand...

1

10 years old, it's my birthday and now I'm getting older
My spine is getting bolder yet my heart is growing colder
It's from the contents of the folder, a divorce, a separation?
I'm fueled with this anger carpet burning from my pacing
My body starts to shaking, who gets despised in this trade
My mother's the defendant and my dad's the one who stayed
He could sense it in my eyes as I cut 'em with the glare
Raised my voice in disbelief, "You know this isn't fair!
How dare you be the plaintiff that's gonna break this family tree!
Have you thought about your son? Have you thought about me!?
I don't think that you can see the way this news affects my life
She's the mother of your child even more she's your wife.
I didn't ask to be here, now you're displacing half my soul.
I don't know your reasons for it, but this couldn've been your goal.
I gotta go, I'm gonna roll before I miss my bus for school.
Happy Birthday to myself, now I'm feeling like a fool!"

This news has riled my ire and I'm trying to hold it in
I'm feeling really tense someone's gonna get done in
The leaf blowing in the wind, it's symbolic of my feelings
I hang my head in shame as I watch the orange peelings
Slide into my foot as the bus hits the breaks
The catalyst of my explosion but it must have been fate
At the end of the orange, a face, she made my heart leap
I wanted to yell but not a peep, I wanted to vent but couldn't speak
All of a sudden I felt a calmness that overcame my body
And a sensation on its trail that made me wanna potty
A true hotty in the sense she's as beautiful as I've seen
The glow around the silhouette whose face is in my dream
I couldn't move a thing as she passed by in the aisle
Our eyes already locked so I blew the girl a smile
The circulation of my blood finally made it to my brain
And the thought I first conjured was I need to know her name
As I hurried to the exit, I lost her in the mass
The second thought that made it was I need to find her class.

Pull your eyes along this line as I peer around the corner
If they knew I skipped homeroom I'm definitely a goner
The mission really simple find the face embedded in my memory
Not one for stalking prey so I hope she just runs into me
How hard could this really be, logic says she's in the building

Demetrius D. Jackson

After the fiascoes at my house, my heart's in need of healing
There's the switch room sounding bell and my eyes are focused, ready
There she is at the end! Now I've gotta keep this steady
Her class is the opposite direction, so I'm feeling like a stalker
As I hop down from my perch my goal is to out walk her
As a means of catching up with her since I'm on the south side
The way she passes through the crowd I can see her legs glide
Ten paces 'til my destination, damn! She dips into her room
Patience, it's a virtue, the ending bell's ringing soon?

I wonder what I did, to make them break their bond
I didn't clean my room and I didn't hug my mom
When she left the other day, out the door, she left for work
And I look just like my dad maybe that's her source of hurt
If she knew I'd give the shirt off my back to prove my love
"Please don't let my mother leave, I'm addressing you above!
I don't want to be the kid from a single-family home
I don't want this separation, please...just leave us alone
If you're listening I'm asking, no I'm begging you for this
If I could do it all over I'd hug and give a kiss
Or I'll do whatever you ask, all you have to do is tell
I guess this ends our session, it's the sounding of the bell."

Back to reality, on my feet, my eyes peer again
A mosaic mass of humanity I have to sort this blend
She's the fifth one out the door, toward the café, she heads for lunch
Tap her shoulder, "A moment of your time if that's not asking you too much?
I noticed you on the bus, and you brightened my dark day
I wanted to address you then but I was speechless and couldn't say
The feeling that flooded my heart, true love right from the start
It takes two to work a union and I hope you'll play your part."

"First of all...who are you? And why are you touching my clothes?
Looks like you need to clean house, in other words go blow your nose
I don't know you and don't want to know you! Love...give me a break!
Us having a union would be the icing on your cake
Next you'll be screaming fate, but it's just not meant to be
You've been told once...now just stay away from me!"

The crowd erupts in laughter, I feel small with a fire burning
Never hit a woman, but she has my stomach turning
I need to turn the other cheek, but my manhood's on the line
If I walk away now they'll swear I have no spine
I'll be a better man for this day, grab a breath of fresh air
Stated, "There's more fish in the sea and I really don't care."

How did it get to this? I got it! I'm still asleep and in a dream
Splash some water on my face and I'll awake from this thing
'Cause see my parents' marriage works, they're as happy as can be
And that outburst from the girl was made up inside of me
Rationalizing was easing the pain until a snicker caught my ear
"The way Carmen told him off it was the headlights and the deer,
I guess she made her point clear from the way he stormed away
Plus the word on the street is he's gay anyway!"

At that point my brain snapped and my eyes arched with rage
As my heart turned black I felt released from a cage
I caught the voice with a hook to the ribs then the jaw
A jab through his glasses, who cares about the law
When he slumped to the ground I stomped a hole through his vest
With him gasping for air, it's the asthmatic's breath
To the ear threw a left cause he was laughing with the voice
Could have kicked him in the knee but the groin was the choice
As he bowed to hold his jewels I aimed for his face
Security guard stopped me by spraying me with mace

Heated, my soul is pacing, while I'm sitting in the chair
My eyes are burning fiercely and this shit ain't fair
I was defamed by the voice and the ear was there as witness
I struck in my name's defense and I'm the one who gets this
Rough and rugged treatment as I'm dragged right through the halls
"His father's on his way" stated the secretary between calls
As if this day couldn't get worse, he's least liked on my list
As I think back to the folder I start to get pissed
At that moment the door parted entering the office it was my dad
With a look of disappointment I couldn't tell if he was mad
He walked back with the principal, ten minutes later I'm called in
She read the list of grievances, I felt like I was in the pen
At the end she reiterated, the zero tolerance policy
Expelled for the year and this decision's to follow me
Handed a bag of belongings and we were both shown the door
Only expelled for the year but I was coming back no more.

The tension was carved with piercing words from my father
They exited upon entry I don't see why he even bothered
Cause the only thing I heard was…a tough road ahead
With blah, blah, blah being the rest that was said
The light in my head was glowing dim with witless comebacks
So instead of useless chatter I hit him with well-known facts
And he disputed nar one, just stated *"We'll discuss this with your mom"*
Turned the corner to see anger with the moving truck on the lawn

Demetrius D. Jackson

Slammed the door, broke the glass, to search the holder of the womb
That carried me for nine, there she sits, the living room
There I stood, not a sound, as I gazed at her she stared
She released the heaviest sigh, so I got myself prepared.

"Honey, come take a seat I know there're answers that you seek
All of them I can't speak but this pendant you should keep
Really close to your heart and you'll know I'm always there
With you in spirit if not physical and I know this isn't fair.
Your dad and I must sort some issues and it's best we're not together
But I'm here for you forever whether rain or snowy weather.
...You're momma's baby boy, but you'll grow to be a man
Believe in your intuition and do the best you can
If you ever need me just call and I'll hold you close again
In this rat race we call life you do what brings the win
Now give momma a hug, stay strong and don't lie
Your word is your bond now wipe those tears from your eyes
I love you with all my heart and it's killing me to leave
My last piece of advice is in yourself always believe."

As she rose from her seat to leave with the last box from the house
I was paralyzed where I sat and as quiet as a mouse
When I heard the door close and reality started to sink
A flood of tears poured and my eyes wouldn't blink
Every bone in my body gave as I collapsed to the floor
It's official my life's over, immediate family's been torn
I wanted her to stop, but no control of this situation
The fact I never saw it coming only added to frustration
First my legs, then my soul, now my heart has started pacing
Trying to fill its void uncertainty's what I'm facing
With my finger no need in placing cause what's done has been done
Maybe just end it now, *where the hell is my father's gun?*
This empty feeling is no fun what did I do to deserve this day
Maybe if I go to sleep this will all just go away.

2

Many of dark nights I cried, many of sunny days I slept
Many of times I wondered why this hasn't settled my soul yet
It's been two years and counting since the obliteration of my world
And the pain hasn't subsided sometimes it makes me wanna hurl
My dad seems to have adjusted, yet I refuse to come to grips
I hate it when he dates…it throws me into fits
It's the pits living this life, time to alter my given path
A heavy heart all this time, I don't think I want it to last.
But where do I turn from here? Every direction I turn is south!
Confusion's what I feel, but confidence comes out my mouth
Maybe I can use the grade change, a transition in my life
Seventh grade a different school, no one knows about my life
I can reinvent this me, and the past no one will see
This change, this is the key I can be all that I can be
But I have to plan accordingly, be careful with reinvention
Don't want to come on too strong, no need for starting tension
Three weeks before it starts, plenty of time to conjure up
This may just be the answer, if I'm having any luck.

My nights turned from self pity to figuring who I wanted to be
Or at least the outside appearance I needed people to see
The adjustments made were mental, an interpretation of myself
On the verge of going insane so I needed this mental health
The first change I felt was crucial observing what's not said
This took a little work to get inside other people's heads
It's more of a read between the lines; I guess I'll make that the second change
I know it's a thin line, that's why I stay in the outer lane
Not one for needing fame, so on my fifteen minutes I'll pass
Be an exemplary student and excel when I'm in class
The last change for now, I'll try to forgive my dad
His marriage is over, he's gonna date, so I need not get mad

Two weeks of polishing my changes after a week of making 'em firm
It's the first day of classes, and this year it's my turn
To walk with my head high, cause everybody here is new
You're the only one who knows so just keep it inside you
Look for Room 122, I guess this will be my homeroom
Grab a seat in the fourth row and a presence seems to loom
I can feel my neck hairs stand, I swear someone's staring me down
A first day ass kicking I'm gone give it to this clown
Need to restrain it's a new year I'm letting my imagination get the best

Demetrius D. Jackson

So I slowly turned around and it was just as I had guessed
Some guy I've never seen with an intent look in my direction
Rose from his seat, he never blinked, and toward me he started stepping

"Hi my name is Tony isn't today a great day?
The sun is shining softly I can't wait to go home and play
Basketball in my backyard, hence the reason why I'm here
We need a sixth man, that's if your schedule's clear
My dad coaches the school team so we practice with 3-on-3
My brother, some of his friends, and then there's just me
They're all in high school now so some nights it gets intense
One night I got my shot blocked over the adjacent fence
Anyway the offer's there just let me know if you'll play
I know it's kind of early so you have 'til the end of the day."

What to say to the offer I felt prostituted for this game
It's only harmless fun plus a friendship to be gained
I weighed my verdict throughout the day and no decision to present
It's the end of the last period and not a moment was spent
Between the ringing of the bell and Tony's appearance at my locker
With this girl who was so sexy if he needs a break then I'll spot her

"So Marcellous what's the deal are we playing in a few
Ah, don't let me be rude let me introduce you two
This is my sister her name's Sasha, Marcellous is in my class."

No more teetering on the fence with that picture of her ass
In those jeans that hugged her hips but not a too tight looking fit
I'm a man I wanted to hit with the bubbling in my pit
"Of course we're going to play just spot me the directions"
I'm guessing in the future her and I can share affections
The first lesson I was taught came in the form of disappointment
So I'm not rushing in this time, I remember the bruises and the ointment

"Here's the directions to my pad we begin about four
We'll already be in the back so no need to pound the door
Just walk right through the gate we'll play 'til about eight
And you're welcome to stay for dinner if that's not being out to late."

With the directions in my palm Sasha and Tony walked away
New school new outlook and he was right…a great day
We lived in the same vicinity so I went home to grab a snack
Left a note attached to the TV, "Gone to ball I'll be back"

At Tony's crib in the backyard, I heard the conversation brewing
What's the teams, was the convo, left everybody stewing
I entered the gate, all eyes gazed, *"Let Marcellous pick his team"*

Apprehensive about the task 'cause I didn't know a thing
About Tony or his family or his brother's high school mates
What if the team I pick brings scrutiny and hate?
I guess I'll play it safe, "I take Tony and his brother"
Agreement was given time to battle one another.

"The game 21, make 'em take 'em, beat by 2
The grass is out of bounds, so you best watch for the doo
Continuation given, only dad can call a foul
If argument ensues then you have to run a mile"

The game rules were agreed upon we shook hands now it's time
For this 3-on-3 contest to commence and unwind:

From Tony's lips it gets intense, so for battle I prepared
They're all older, the opposition, but my heart's not beating scared
I threw myself into this trance state to bring a higher level…
Fueled from worlds beyond, thought my soul sold to the devil
First on defense I had the guard from the varsity squad
Who beat me only once on a back door lob
From then on he hit two shoots 'cause I didn't beat the pick
That no one ever called out so that really made me sick
Now on offense that was my lick, an out of body experience
Fluid water is how I flowed while the defense was feeling tense
Guarding me was impossible I was the shadow you couldn't see
Draining jumper after jumper I was the rain on their forest tree
I had my hand in a few assists and pulled a rebound here and there
Noticed Sasha noticing me as she twirled her jet black hair
After all was said we were 8 and 2 then I flipped the switch to ease
The other team, winded with their hands upon their knees
Congratulations from my team on a game well played
I had built a nice appetite, dinner was offered so I stayed

Tony's mother made a roast, potatoes, with green beans on the side
With my performance in the backyard I was feeling a sense of pride

"Wow Marcellous, that showing was great and that wasn't against slouches
They've decimated many people, sent 'em crying back to their houses
And the defense you played on Reggie, he's looking at being All-State
You shut him down mercilessly now he's gotta eat off that plate
Maybe you should go out for the team, I told you my dad's the coach
He was telling my mom about your game and he's not the type to boast."

At that moment his dad reentered the room, *"Marcellous, Tony is right.*
I'm intrigued by the way you handled yourself out on the court tonight
I'd love to have you as part of the team, you'd make a nice addition
Currently we have a vacancy at the shooting guard position."

Hmm, I never really thought about basketball or organized sports
But I did feel invigorated while I was out there on the court
"The offer is great, why don't you let me sleep on what you suggest
I need some time to evaluate, I'll have an answer in the morning at best."

After dinner concluded I thanked the Joneses for dinner and their hospitality
During the walk back to my crib the proposition kind of rattled me
What does it mean to my future if I'm successful in this quest?
Do I have the fortitude to give it may all...my best?
This thought plagued me for the rest of the night, I can't seem to think on my feet
I said that I would sleep on it, so I guess I'll drift to sleep.

3

"Hustle boys! Hustle! This ain't no cupcake drill
Pain equals gain, that's what your legs are starting to feel
This year we need to dominate from defense to fatigue
We need to finish the games strong and we'll win the city league!"

Coach Jones was really though, but to win that is his passion
During practice he's the chief no time for joking or laughing
We were his tribe of Indians following what we're told
He had a master plan and we each had to play our roles
It was three days before our first game, my dad doesn't even know
I've gone out for the team and I'm the main show
My reasons for not telling him, I'm not sure I even have 'em
I'm sure he'll be shocked 'cause three months ago I didn't fathom
I'd be in this predicament, now I'm making myself a name
For me it's just a release, not one for needing the fame
With the looming of the game it's time to inform him now
I can still hardly believe it myself, I wonder how it will sound.

No time is like the present, my thought entering the door
Heard the TV from my Father's room, dropped my bag on the floor
Climbed the fourteen steps 'til my moment of truth, but how to pass the news
It was never stated I couldn't so I couldn've broke a rule
Nevertheless an uneasy feeling was darkening my steps
Words to formulate a sentence I was giving it my best
Yet the more I formed, the worst I felt, excuses is what they were
Tools of incompetence to build structures of nothingness flashed in a blur
Opened the door it was her, a woman, straddled over his hips
I spotted them, they spotted me, then my stomach did back flips
I think I'm gon' get sick, towards the bathroom I moved with haste
The expression on their face, like I was intruding in this place
The lid was down I grabbed the basket of waste and hurled my eyes bloodshot
My throat was feeling raw, while my nose was filled with snot
From my eyes' corner I could spot my dad's figure in the hall
Entering the bathroom and shutting the door, trying not to fall

"Son I'm sorry you walked in on me and the next door neighbor
I was asked to do her a favor, before I knew it erotic behavior
With the details I will spare you, but you really should have knocked
Now all three of us are feeling awkward, but you put her on the spot
If Andy was to find out, well let's just pray he never does
But if he does their marriage is through and it's he that she loves
It was a one time thing, I promise it'll never happen again

Demetrius D. Jackson

I broke through vows and the sanctity of marriage, I'll work with God for my sins..."

Somehow the words didn't matter, because my gut had a different feeling
With my finger I couldn't place it, but there's more he's not spilling
I glanced at him momentarily, "I'm on the basketball team.
Our first game is on Friday, you don't have to come or anything
I thought I would just inform you, so now my job is done
Go on back to your madam I really have to run"

Picked myself up from the bathroom deck, through the door, down the steps
His marriage was a wreck so he'll ruin someone else's what the heck
I couldn't stay in the house, I decided to go to Tony's place
They were like family, with them I've always felt safe

It was nearing the end of October and the weather was beginning to shift
A woman passerby saw me walking and asked if I needed a lift
I declined she went on her way five minutes later I was there
I knocked on the door, Sasha opened it up, I couldn't help but stare
"Hey Sasha, how are you doing? Is Tony home by chance?"
"He and my parents went to the store." I've always wanted to get in her pants.
"You're more than welcome to wait, I'm just sitting here alone
Live company is always better than just chatting on the phone"

I decided to wait, we entered the living room, Jeopardy was on the tube
"Where are my manners, would you like something to drink, I didn't mean to be rude"
Water is fine, she bounced away, composure is my thought
Stop staring before you're caught, bring this nonsense to a halt
The speaking angels advice wasn't bought, when she reentered I was at it again
She sat down in front of me, *"The game this Friday, you think you'll win?"*
I believed it to be a strong possibility, but I told her "I'm not sure
I heard their defense is really tough, it may be hard to score"
"Well I'm sure you'll do great, afterwards you and I can commemorate
I already know you have eyes for me so we'll call it our first date."
At that moment she leaned over and kissed me, her hand massaging my crotch
"If you really think you're ready, come to my locker I'll tell you the spot"

The keys jingling in the door, Sasha bit my lower lip
Gently, not in a rush, the lock was giving someone a fit
She slithered back to the couch as the door slid open
I wanted her right then, and my body wasn't copin'
Tony's family broke the mood I've longed for since we met
If something was to happen it'd be the quietest secret ever kept

The night moved on I stayed for dinner, Tony and I played PS2
Chemistry was building between Sasha and I, no one had a clue
The prospect of her proposal made me wish for shorter days

Or proposed longer stays while her family is away
However and nonetheless my time was spent, I left for home
To spend the night in my room, cold and all alone.

Finally a wish come true, It's Friday night a quarter 'til eight
During shoot around I didn't notice my dad he may be running late
It's fifteen minutes 'til the start, tonight I have to hit my zone
Have a good all-around game, then with the win we'll go home

Dribble handoff now I'm isolated right wing
I beat him to the baseline all day he wouldn't dream
Desperation in his eyes, he's gonna take his shot
The moment that he reaches, the motion hits a stop...

Now I damage his soul with the cross
Between the legs twice his center of gravity is off
Two hard dribbles to the right, he stumbles to keep pace
He does his best not to be fooled in this place
Here comes his reoccurring nightmare his psyche has been psyched
He's been trained all day so it's hard for him to fight
He overprotects the boundary, but I cross to hit the middle
He looks shocked, now he wishes he was at home with his pillow
He's riddled now his teammates scurry in defense
It's crazy they've never seen a man this intense
Their center, their last hope, between me and scoring two
I eye him up and down as to say, *Whatcha gonna do?*
Calf flexing, thundering off the ground now in mid flight
Their center stuck and dumbfounded caught in awe at the sight
Cock the ball back with authority, I swear I'm trying to kill it
Mass times acceleration now the entire block can feel it

At the conclusion of the game, during the celebration with my team
At my locker there sat a cop and I'm wondering *what does all this mean?*
The look on his face was solemn and my heart began to worry
"Marcellous Thompson I presume?" He went on to tell his story:

"The call came in about 7:30 a horrible wreck at an intersection
The cars hit head on, one going the wrong direction
I was the first response on the scene, the driver of one car DOA
I headed to the other car, he was hurt in a bad way
All he kept saying was, 'My son, it's his first basketball game'
He told me the name of the school, Marcellous Thompson was the name
The passenger, a younger lady, was thrown from the car
She managed broken bones only after being thrown so far
But I'm sad to say your father's condition was far worse

Demetrius D. Jackson

He didn't make it, as for the lady we found ID in her purse
From what I can tell you all were neighbors, I'm sorry to bear this news
We still need you to ID the body, I'm sorry it's your father you had to lose"

Crushed and speechless, I couldn't assimilate what he just said
A two car accident as a result my father is now dead
There must be some mistake, this equation doesn't balance
Maybe there's another Marcellous Thompson, my brain can't fit around this
I began to feel light headed, the salty tears found my mouth
Shock had taken over and immediately I passed out

4

"It's breakfast boys and girl!" A sound I got quite use to hearing
The last year of high school, a college decision is quickly nearing
On my way down the stairs to the breakfast table Sasha gave me a wink
Normally meant I want you tonight, let me know what you think
Since the death of my father, five years ago, the Jones family took me in
They couldn't seem to find my mother so this was a win-win
Under the guidance of Mr. Jones, I was the top player in the state
Many colleges recruited me fiercely, I had a decision to make
But not right now it's time for breakfast, I'm as hungry as can be
Sasha made her way to the table slyly eye balling me

It still puzzles me how we never got caught having sex in her room or mine
We've done it at least once a month and it was close from time to time
Yet somehow we managed to keep this secret Sasha keeps me on my toes
Trying things she saw on flicks while watching industry pros
Tonight I'm sure it'd be no different but I've gotta wean her loose
She's the only one I've been with, she's that good, I'm telling you the truth
This in-house "lust affair" must soon come to a close
We're following different paths, something everybody knows
I guess tonight, strong I'll stand, I will have to tell her no
It's never been done before so I'll see how that will go

"Mrs. Jones thank you for breakfast again, as usual you've outdone yourself
I'm telling you, you should open a shop, it'll bring you fortunes and wealth"
Something I suggested many of times, yet knowing she wouldn't bite
Kissed her on the cheek as I made my exit, "I'll be home late tonight"
I was going to use some time in the evening to plan my college tour
I had narrowed my choice to three schools time to see what they have in store
Strangely enough the thing that swayed me the most was educational prowess
Basketball is fine and dandy but a degree will allow this
Boy with a humble background to provide for himself
And his family in the future with physical and mental health
The schools on the list definitely had an education to boast
And one of these final three in the end, with me they'll toast
But first things first a college visit to see where I'll reside
With education and basketball the backdrop, what else could they provide

After hours of intense preparation, a plan formulated at last
I'll make college rounds once we make it out of class
For the Christmas holiday, I'll swing through the institutions
It's time to take this serious and that is no disputing
Not sure for which I'm rooting, but at the conclusion I'll decide

Demetrius D. Jackson

The makings of a road trip I'll see if Tony wants to ride
He's always been by my side, so it'll pain me when we part
That's why I want him to venture with me so he'll see this as a start
Of us growing and maturing plus he'll have some place to visit
I'm not gonna turn my nose to spite him or seek for things exquisite
It'll be a riveting experience shared between best friends
And the stories we'll tell our grandkids while sitting in our dens

As I made my way back to the house, my thoughts swirled in the wind
Stopped to reflect on my life asked God for his ear to lend
Dear Lord you've given me hurdle after hurdle to overcome
In my life I feel it's not right yet I stand refusing to run
I've endured many a tragedy that's turned others sour
Success is only in your granting power, thus I pray to you every hour
But sometimes I wonder if you cower, believe me, I believe
The lost of my father I can't conceive, but you were there to help me grieve
What was the 'everything happens' behind that sleeve I guess only time will tell
I just pray for a brighter future and that everything goes well.

Snapped out of my trance-like spell to open the front door of the house
Sasha was sitting on the love seat wearing a see-through pink colored blouse
And some jeans to accentuate her hips with a light gloss to show her lips
Coconut and Lime was the scent that was throwing my hormones into fits
My teeth began to grit as I tried to fight these lustful feelings
Our connection was only physical my heart she wasn't stealing
Yet I'm reeling and it's killing me to break off what we share
But to her this isn't fair so I recline into the chair
She can sense it in the glare that I give when our eyes connect
A tear trickles down her cheek and I haven't spoken yet
Is this something I'll regret? Nonetheless I must proceed
Kiddy gloves is what I need 'cause she's delicate indeed

"Sasha we've moved at lighting speed, but it's time we pull the reins
It's something we knew would come and it pains me all the same
See there's nothing more we can gain with our pending separation
When it's college I'll go and junior year you'll be facing
And there's really no need in chasing 'cause you'll be wasting an opportunity
To have a loving relationship there's nothing more I'd rather see
And honestly the sex was great, you'll definitely please your mate
You're no slouch or second rate, but it's time we call the break."

The trickling tear turned to a stream but she was silent as she wept
Was I right to do this now? How much pain will she get?
At that moment I wanted to forget every word that I just uttered
Until Sasha raced off the couch and with a hug began to smother
Every doubt or second guessing for the words that I just spoke

22

It was a hug of agreement and a willingness to cope.
She professed she had one hope that, *"...tonight would be our last.*
We have the house to ourselves so no need to make it fast."

Hesitant about this moment but once more could do no harm
So I lead her up the stairs when I grabbed her by the arm:

It's round one scheduled for three but the distance we're not traveling
The intensity from the start had her moaning between babbling
The bed sheets she started grappling while the wall she tried to climb
And it wasn't in her mind, it's the tingling in her spine
It was a learning experience during our time, I learned the spots that drove her quick
Lick the inner portion of the thigh and with the tongue a quick flick
Of the clit, it gave her fits and caused a breakage of the dam
Then she demanded I roll over all I said was, "Yes Ma'am"
She stroked my membrane and moistened it good then she straddled for the ride
She got intense spotting her reflection in the mirror on the side
The impact when we collide caused motion from the bed
Got mesmerized with the action so I watched her bobbing head
My ego was being fed when she screamed my name with Jesus
It was a presence in the room so I'm sure somebody see's this
It's the moment, I can't believe this, she unmounts to drink it all
It wasn't small, she's on the ball, she didn't pull away or stall
The bed caught her on her fall and she was cradled in the sheets
Exhausted, we both were so we drifted off to sleep.

5

"...you thought your secret would skip my eye, then you're more foolish than I thought
I walked in on y'all your second time, that's when you got caught
It was the thing that I most fought, my sister being diddled by my friend
And you sexed her and she sexed you again and again
You placed me in a no win so for y'all's security I bartered
I'd be the man on lookout the moment y'all got started
But the trade Sasha made was her services before my shower
At the time you were asleep and my parents raced to catch the working hour
It was a tremendous type of power so I guess it's you I have to thank
The way she rode it, she could hold it when it was her ass I had to spank."

Shock over took my conscience I couldn't believe what I just heard
My eyes focused on the road again in time to miss the squatting bird
"Tony that's absurd! Man Sasha is your sister
I never should have slept with her and then you couldn've pushed her
That wasn't a barter, it was blackmail, you're Satan's forgotten son
You might as well ripped her panties and hit it while holding a gun
I bet you thought it was fun..."

"This is the police pull over!"
The flashing light in my rearview thank God that I'm sober
What's the reason for the stoppage, my thoughts swirling swiftly
I could try to floor it but that's a little risky
So I descend and pull over a second P.O. comes from the front
I glance over at Tony, "Looks like they're on a hunt"
Placed both hands on the steering wheel, no misunderstanding to be made
Not trying to be laid out on the concrete freshly paved
One officer approached on the passenger side, hand close tucked to the hip
Another on the drivers side with a toothpick hanging from his lip
I tighten up my grip, the officer flashlight taps my window
He motions to roll it down, his hat shifts with the wind blow

"Son I pulled you over do you know the reason for
I'm gon' need you to step out the car won't you open up the door
Any drugs on the floor, any weapons on your person
Can you open up the trunk we need to do some searchin'
We had reports of rash robberies, what's your purpose in our state
You're in Texas now boy, you need a front license plate
Your buddy looks suspicious, 'Tommy keep an eye on that nigger...'"

What the fuck! Damn it was exactly as I figured!

At that point I realized they weren't gonna play this by the books
Assumptions already made that me and Tony are crooks
"Officer look, I'm leaving from the university as a guest
They're recruiting me to play ball cause they know that I'm the best
We're not involved in the robbery mess, so we'll just be on our way
So you and Tommy can move on and enjoy the rest of your day."

"You're not going nowhere boy, 'Hey you get out the car'
'Tommy cuff him up, so you're a rising star?
Well here you're not going far, I don't want you in my city
There's no one for miles around so no one will pay you pity"

On cue Tommy began to beat Tony with the handle of his stick
When his body hit the ground, with his boot he began to kick
I couldn't believe this shit, the officer had his gun to my head

"If you come to my city again, you and your friend will end up dead."

He took the butt of his gun and hit me, I collapsed to taste the dirt
Uncuffed Tony and walked away I could tell that he was hurt
As they drove off I gathered myself, walked over to the passenger side
The damage they did to Tony I nearly broke down and cried
The anger I felt inside, I could feel the bubbling in my pit
The injustice in this "just" world, this is something I won't forget
Profusely blood poured from his lips, I reached down to pick him up
I couldn't tell if he was conscious because his eyes were closed shut
"With any luck there's an emergency room nearby, cause Tony you need some help"
I've seen racism in life before, but this is the worst I've ever felt
Tony began to speak, *"Man just get us away from here."*
He reached and grabbed his side from his eye he shed a tear

I put the car in gear and headed for the state line
Once we break the boundary I'll look for the hospital sign
Thoughts began racing through my mind, *How could people be so callous?*
Yeah slavery is over yet there's racism all about us
This is the only air we breathe, and we all need it to live
Yet we can't coincide and have a helping hand to give
The world has turned it's back and all snakes have shed their skin
If a vote was cast today a majority would want slavery again
Then swear up and down it's not a sin, justifiable they'll rationalize
I've gotta make a way for myself and not falter to their demise.

The hospital's the next right, Tony's breathing is getting shallow
He's been my friend a long time his actions I couldn't fathom
But right now his safety's my only concern, I hope I'm not late
Emergency room is on the left I fly right through the gate

Demetrius D. Jackson

Hop out the ride, run inside, "Help my friend is dying!"
Two orderlies swooped around the corner almost as if they were gliding
They grabbed a gurney placed Tony on it, and I followed in a rush
All eyes upon our entrance, all spectators watched with a hush
"Son these forms are a must, we'll take care of your friend
Bring them to the counter once you reach the end."

I hurried through the forms, "Nurse what's my friend's condition?"
"Some internal bleeding, some broken ribs, and a tooth has come up missing"

She continued to speak but it was hard to listen, the knot on my head was throbbing
The last thing I remember before I blacked out was somebody's toddler sobbing

6

The biggest day in my young life the auditorium rumors are buzzing
Overhear a side convo, *"Man Marcellous is my cousin."*
Amazed at how all the fussing is centered around me today
A press conference, my college decision, and I don't know what I'm gon' say
However, I know where I won't play, back in the town of them racist bastards
Three months for Tony to recover fully after a pint of his blood was plastered
On the streets and on their sticks, if I could control the hands of time
I'd go back to that scene and all vengeance would be mine
But I've got to clear my mind, articulate and speak with wisdom
A decision is what they crave and that's exactly what I'm gon' give 'em
Our head coach is at the podium, I place one foot in front of the other
As I climb the creaking stairs I think of my father and my mother
I do it every day and this day won't differ from the rest
As he finishes my introduction, I compose myself with a deep breath

"Good afternoon and thank you for coming, I guess I'll get right to the business
As a kid growing up I definitely didn't foresee this
And now with the moment here I can hardly believe it's happening
It's been an arduous bumpy ride almost broke the seatbelt fastening
Nonetheless I stand before you ready to take the next step
The life of a college athlete, how much better does it get
I'm going to take this opportunity at this institution of higher learning
I choose Tha Syndicate University, that is where my heart is burning..."

The crowd erupted in cheers as I placed on the school's cap
High school coach nodded his head and gave the approval clap
Tony and his parents were visible in the front rows
While Mrs. Jones shed a tear and blew in her tissue to clear her nose
I could see the recruiter on the phone verifying my conformation
To my surprise my new head coach was there with a slight smile of elation
For once my heart quit pacing and caressed a steady rhythm
As I realized the "family" I'm leaving behind my success is what I'll give them.

I make my way down the stairs a back pat here a high-five there
The scene was surreal, not a butt left in the chairs
At that moment I had no cares I felt as free as the blowing wind
I make my way to the Jones family to give them hugs once again
Mrs. Jones' tears streaming to her chin and a little mist for the mister
I gave Tony a hug while being eyeballed by his sister

*"A celebration party tonight and no is not an option
It's already been planned all you have to do is stop in."*

I guess Tony's feeling better if he partook in the planning for this outing
So I won't put up a fight no need to drag me kicking and shouting
Yet I could sense Sasha pouting, so I slid by Tony to grant her a hug
She whispered in my hear, *"Though we're through it's you I love."*
Kissed me on the cheek, took a step back and then continued to clap
I then made my way back to my new coach shortly after that

The remainder of the day moved without incident with anticipation of the evening
I could still hardly believe in a few months I'd be leaving
I took a few moments to gather myself in convincing it'll all be okay
Just don't get ahead of yourself and live to seize the day

"Hey Marcellous! Man come on! It'd be nice to leave before it's dawn
Plus we got an extension on our curfew I cleared it with my mom
You know she's not one to cave, hurry up before she flips
And realizes she agreed to two and proclaim that 'yes' was a slip
Need I remind you, did you forget this is your celebration
You're on the verge on missing it all, that's an angry mob you'll be facing
Plus all the bu..."

"Alright, alright, don't get your panties in a bunch
I had to analyze my beard I think I trimmed away too much
But let's go ahead and dip, yeah I'm ready to enjoy this night
A mixture with a college crowd I bet it'll be out of sight"

As we made our way due south I could feel the house base thumping
When we entered through the door yo that motha' was straight jumping
The energy pulsating, pumping, the nice flare with the disco light
Even had a cage dancer man I tell you it was hype
And the mixture was just right 1.5 for every man
Plus they came in a wide variety, yeah they covered every span
Grabbed a punch with the right hand as I peered over the crowd
People on the dance floor, grinding getting wild
The DJ pushed the volume loud and the crowd got more intense
There's no way you'd hold up the wall or be caught straddling the fence
This is a dream I need a pinch but...I never fell asleep
The floor boards must be weak, I could feel them shifting under my feet.
At the conclusion of my blink I noticed a redbone staring
Her lips parted words I couldn't hear, the music's blaring
But I could read those beautiful lips, *"Do you wanna go upstairs?"*
Contemplated for a moment then I thought who would care
So I nodded with agreement and followed through her path
Up the twelve stairs, the corner room, we arrived there at last
The bass had the room shaking but the treble kept the voices low
She was audible enough I heard, *"I've watched from the door*

'Til the moment you felt my stare, it's nice to finally meet
The man's who's smile just made my body weak"
I could tell she was on the creep but how far am I willing to go
My press conference was today her eyes could be seeing dough
But I couldn't tell her no I wanted to see where her head was at
So I played her little game and said, "Is that a matter of fact?
I don't just hop in the sack, but I'm down for getting knowledge
We can treat this bedroom like our own personal cottage."

Right on cue she unbuckled my belt and button proceeded to unzip
Slid my pants down to my ankles and slowly licked her lip
Dropped my boxers prepared to grip when yelling hysteria broke out
The DJ's music stopped everyone was running out the house
A loud bang was heard, *was that a shot?* "Girl we gotta go!"
Not chancing it through the house we opt the window instead of the doo'
"What they shootin' foo'?" Some shit is always going down
We sprinted through the town once we made it to the ground
She stated her house was around the corner, so I decided to walk her home
She asked me to come in but the mood for me was gone
Something's always going wrong, the thought pounding in my head
I just need to get home and crawl into the bed

Made it home greeted by a hug by Mrs. Jones, who looked worried
Tony came around the corner, *"At the first shot man I scurried*
I waited outside for a half when you didn't show I figured you were here
Moms wouldn't let me back out for the worst she began to fear"

I could tell he was sincere, but the worst they've yet to tell
Turns out someone got shot and died, *Man what the hell?*
I could hardly believe this turn of events motionless without a speech
Finally I decided enough is enough, went up the stairs and went to sleep.

7

I've always hated saying goodbye since the day my mother left
Almost eight years ago I still remember hyperventilating for a breath
But this goodbye has different terms, I'm leaving now for college
The way the Joneses took me in I show them nothing but homage
A big step into this cruel world, however not quite fully submerged
I'll need to find my niche and soar with the eagles not the birds

"Hello… Earth to Marcellous! We're trying to take this picture
A recent photo in the house, but it's not like we'll forget ya
Now everybody say cheese…"

Mr. Jones and his camera
I remember Mrs. Jones threatened to break it with a hammer
They're a lively little bunch, I couldn't have found a better place to stay
It's kind of sad in a way, that I'm about to go away

"Marcellous you've been really quiet is everything alright?"

"I'm just thinking how much you all mean to me before I take this flight
You've done so much for me, thank you just doesn't seem enough
You were my guardian angels when things really got rough
Not to sound mushy and stuff but I love all of you
You've really turned my life around in case you didn't have a clue
Now I'm grown up making a true journey away from home
Where I'll be ninety percent of the time, kind of all alone
I can reach out and dial the phone, the home cooking will be missed
When you send a care package put your cookies on the list
All of that to say this I appreciate what all that you've done
I think of you as my parents hopefully you think of me as your son."

"Of course we do son, you've been a welcomed addition
Don't think you are alone, we'll do plenty of missing
We knew this day would come, we're prepared to let you go
Our house is always your home, in case you didn't know
Now go ahead and get on your plane, call us when you arrive"
"You have a strong will, we know you will survive."

We all hugged and said our goodbyes, then I boarded my plane
Sure I'm going to ball but college isn't a game
Got to be studious during the fame, always stay a step ahead
God forbid something should happen, got to have the knowledge in my head
Where's a bed when you need one, I could definitely use a nap
Nah, I'll use this time to prepare my next transition for my map.

COLLEGE

8

"I ain't got nothing, we're going board!" That's the third time tonight
Playing spades, the dorm tourney, it's the middle of the night
My partner's steamed ready to fight, the card Gods have played us cruel
Thursday flips to Friday, tomorrow I have no classes at the school
Conversation's the cash pool from which I quickly divert my attention
The bet's on Saturday's game for which I'm the starter, not to mention
It's against all the rules for me to be involved in such a convo
Get suspended for allegations then on the bench, ride the pine hell no!
Thus I quickly displace their attention on Kristina entering the lobby
She's sexy, kind of smart, but stuck up and extremely snobby

"For her action I would rob B, the president and his staff
A life bid I'm willing to risk if it means I tap that ass."

Marlo...he's from New York and his loins are always fiending
Since last year he's constantly lusted Kristina, awakening from his dreams screaming
"Kristina don't leave me, you know I love you boo!"
The first night it happened we didn't know what to do
So we closed his mouth with glue, he'll never live that down
Despite his intelligence he can really be a clown
Chris smacks the table with a pound, *"Gentleman that's game!"*
We got our asses handed to us, my parents would be ashamed

"Y'all cats is still lame, next week we take revenge
We'll send you home crying to your moms in her Depends"

Marlo tends to go over the deep end, but we know it's for fun and laughter
Maybe he shed insight on himself 'cause he has a weak bladder
Now to the heart of the matter, mental preparation for the game
My knee's been hurting me, time to block away the pain
Remember why you came and the reason you are here
A daily reminder to myself something I need to hear
Failure in life is my biggest fear, that keeps me motivated
I'll have a successful career once I've graduated
Even if basketball doesn't pan out, I've got the fall-back plan
Thinking responsibly is the first step to becoming a man
Nonetheless press play on the VCR, channel 3, the TV Station
The opposing team's video to watch to complete my preparation.

Two days of intense preparation the tip-off's almost here
Mentally recite the game plan to ensure I have it clear

I veer into my alter state to visualize every play
Yet there's a disturbance deep inside, refusing to go away
The ball's on it's way up, we control the initial tip
I position myself right wing, noticeably I start to limp
Marcellous get a grip... My internal words of wisdom
The point guard calls for a pick so I go out and give him
An open path through the lane, mid range "J" he sticks for two
Momentarily the pain subsides as adrenaline comes through

Twenty game minutes, this internal battle, thirty-five ticks on the clock
Feels like two bones are rubbing, I'll check at half, no need to stop
Just as I'm dishing off the rock I collapse at mid-court
A sensation shoots up my spine, I'm in pain of all sorts
My knee is engulfed in flames I beat the floor my mind worries
The ref stops the play the medical staff comes in a hurry
There's a flurry of thoughts, none process, visions of the worst

"Where's the pain son?" The question that was asked first.

"Doc it's my knee...ah...I don't know it feels on fire"

His expression became solemn, the situation must be dire
He motions to the bench, two of my teammates come to assist
The disgust I felt inside, nearly broke my knuckles clinching my fist
"Doc what's the meaning of this?" *"Just a precautionary measure*
No need to antagonize the injury your knee we need to treasure."

There is no pleasure in this pain as I'm carried off the floor
Pass the bench, through the tunnel, to x-ray behind the door
My emotions began to pour, "Doc will I play again?
Will I be back on the court tonight to celebrate our win?"
Confused message with his grin, *"Marcellous I'm not sure"*
Coach Johnson interrupted with the banging on the door

"Doc I'm interested, what's his knee's prognosis?"

"It's too early to tell, to ease the pain I gave him doses
Of pain killers that reduces swelling after the game I'll report
My intuition says don't expect him back on the court."

Damn twist of cruel fate, again I bury the anger deep inside
Peace and anger tugging at me, but they're ready to collide
In the aftermath I better hide, the anger grows with more power
Turbulence at every turn is making my heart sour
For now I have it capped, but it's bubbling trying to explode
If it ever reaches the top I fear it's something I can't hold
Semblance of composure that's my mode, this feeling I'll shake
I have to! I didn't take this journey to make a mistake

The doctor fitted me with crutches while eyeballing my results
The dilation in his pupils said the words he never spoke
I could feel his brain massaging words, to pass the bad news.
He wouldn't be able to fix me, I read the context clues
"Doc just give it to me straight, how long am I out?"
"*The rest of the year*" Were the words out his mouth
I could sense me going south, hung my head in disbelief
"*Marcellous it gets worse, sorry to add to your grief.*
This damage has been lingering, surgery is weeks overdue
Seems you've been ripping at a tendon is this the first it bothered you?"

"There's been a nagging pain for months, but never like this
I figured it was wear from the games, I would never risk
An injury to this extent, wait...to what is this extent

"*You'll never play again.*" All the air in my lungs went
Evaporating into the darkness I could feel my heart stop
I could feel the anger prop while my jaw had to drop
"Acceptable this is not, damn it run the test again"
"*It's been run three times and the same results were turned in.*"
Right then I felt like the little boy on my tenth day of birth
Is there justice in this cruel world, what's it really worth?
Subside my anger first before my pain reverts to action
This news was very taxing, who's the leader of this faction
That perpetuates this cloud that's constantly above my life
If not for my belief in Christ, it'd be simpler to take a knife
Just one vein a quick splice, I could feel the Devil lurk
Tuck away the hurt, I'll find a way to make this work.

"Doc I apologize. Does the coach know?
If he doesn't could you tell him, I really need to go."

Grabbed my crutches, through the door, exited stage left
"I'll still find a way" I muttered under my breath.

9

Three weeks since the season ended, we barely clipped the five hundred mark
We were present at every game yet, our play lacked heart
I tried to do my part giving insight from my studies
Yeah they're all my buddies, but the waters ran muddy
I had enough to think about with my Chem test looming
A hard one I'm presuming, this class is definitely dooming
My chances of progressing gracefully this is my second stint
The first failure was all my fault, primarily I never went
Certainly put a dent in my invincibility academically
Won't hurt me too much, it's just what it all meant to me

The phone rings when I answer it's the coach on the other end
"Marcellous I'm in my office would you mind coming in?"
"Sure I'll be right over." *What's the nature of this call?*
I hang up, throw on some shoes then proceed to the hall
This makes no sense at all, I don't understand the meaning
My gut says it's not right I could feel the balance leaning
This equation seems unbalanced, only a constant will even
This inequality, and the dark cloud isn't leaving
A swinging array of emotions as I darken the door frame
The athletic director also seated, I'm summoned by name

"Marcellous come have a seat, be sure to close the door."

Any easiness I felt absolutely I had no more
I read it in Coach Johnson's eyes, the mood of the room shifted
The bubbling started to stir and the anger was getting lifted

*"Son you're really gifted, it's an unpleasant circumstance
To lose you how we lost you, was a kick right in the pants
We'll recoup that's our stance, and a tough decision was made
We keep arriving at this conclusion, no matter how we swayed
You were marvelous when you played, now that chapter's closed
We can endure no more hardship our funding is taking blows
Thus we brought you to this meeting before the papers arrived
We had to cut your scholarship, you no longer have a ride
They've repacked what they could we're sorry to cut you loose
You'll always be family, Marcellous that's the truth."*

They couldn't look me in my face, my glare could have split 'em
My impulse was to lash out, revenge I need to get 'em
"What the hell am I to do now, I can't afford this shit."

Demetrius D. Jackson

A tear permeated my eye, *Marcellous get a grip*
But the more I tried to calm myself the angrier I became
On the verge of going insane, there's a pressure in my brain
Out coach's window I could see the rain, a fitting atmosphere
I could feel the darkness cloud my heart, realization of my fear
The overflow was taking place I feel I'm losing control
All this built up agony was beginning to take it's toll
For my goals and ambitions, they're now swirling down the drain
Rational thought took a backseat, I was thinking with my pain

"Marcellous, we obtained your package, this is where you stand
Again we're sorry son, we've done the best we can."

Snatched the paper from his hand, forced my way out the office
Am I the one to blame. Am I the reason I lost this.
At this point it didn't matter gathered my attention to the paper
Thirty-one hundred due in two weeks, *not without a caper*

With this new anger my mind wandered, *I'm not leaving school*
You're going to be an engineer, problem solving is what you do
As much as my inner voice knew it was wrong, anger took over
The inner ten-year-old recreates the pain inside that folder

Went to my room grabbed my winter gear, it's a raining 65
Just the gloves, mask, skully cap, and the keys for the ride
The angel was losing the battle inside the devil turned the key
It was an out of body experience in third person watching me
In and out, in and out, the words pounding in my head
All color seemed to fade and matriculated into red
Assembled the gear to their proper places, car's around the block
My conscience knows the steps I'm taking, yet helpless to stop
This quickly orchestrated plan from acting, it's the campus bank

The teller saw me turn the corner, surprised she didn't faint
One guard has always been the norm, today it was the same
Dusted him with a two piece exclaimed, "This ain't a game!
Give me all the cash, dammit everybody else on the floor"
Quickly made the adjustment to lock the entering door
The manager looked unsure 'til I grabbed the teller's head
"Make the wrong move, you'll ensure that she's dead
Now get your ass over here fill the bag I ain't got time to waste"
In and out, in and out, leave the money in the safe
The bag was filled with the teller's drawers, I released the girl
While bolting for the lobby doors I could hear her hurl
Almost home make my way to the car, what the fuck is this
Turned the corner to my car being jacked, didn't have time to be pissed
A barrel found the small of my back, *"Hand over the bag!"*

My well-formed calculated plan has run into a snag
Now my anger was getting mad, but they had the upper hand
Frustrated with my choices, I released the bag from my hand
"Thank you, a wise decision, now how hard was that?"
A shot fired, I could smell my flesh, a bullet pierced my back

10

Groggy and full of pain when I awake from my sleep
Not quite sure of my surroundings and I'm feeling very weak
Then I notice the IV, *I'm in a hospital room?!*
What's the reason for this, I hope a memory surfaces soon
Yet memory clouds tend to loom, then the door swings open
Maybe someone with answers that's all that I'm hoping

*"You're awake how are you coping? You are a strong kid
Not many people pull through surgery the way that you did."*

"Miss I don't mean to be impatient but, why am I here?"

*"Honey you were shot in the back, but you have nothing to fear
You'll be on your feet in a month or so, with some rehabilitation
A small uphill battle is the situation that you're facing."*

Right then it hit, my actions, my gloves, my mask
The robbery, my car, do I dare even ask
Do I need to flee? At this point I am confused
How could I have been so stupid I have everything to lose

"Somebody's got a visitor." Coach entered the room slow.
Paranoia began to grip, *How much does he know?*

"Marcellous son how are you?" He gave me a slight glare

"I've definitely felt better but for now I guess I'm fair"

*"Marcellous I was driving by when I heard a shot fired
I stopped, when the body hit the ground I figured I was tired
His clothes were similar to the ones you had on in my office
The thoughts that ran through my head, I damn near lost it
I rushed to your aid the situation felt tense
Blood splattered on the ground, in the grass, on the fence
Quick to call the ambulance, put some pressure on your back
Said a prayer, the medics showed up shortly after that
I'm just glad that you will make it, 'everything' will be okay
I have some articles of yours I'll just keep them tucked away."*

Articles?! Could he possibly mean *my mask and my gloves*
The configuration of his sentence, I'm positive he does
That's where our conversation stopped, the nurse came calling
*"It's time for your rehab we can't afford to have you falling
This is Jasmyn she's responsible for getting you on your feet*

It's a vow that you took and a promise she will keep."

I could have sworn I was asleep, she had a simplistic beauty
I sensed my heart flutter, mentally rubbed my eyes, still a cutie
But I'm in no mood to be flirting, courting, or even dating
Coach's comments were on my mind and that's no debating.
Concerned is understating, but a distraction may be what I need
I'll just take it day by day and see where things lead.

"Hi Marcellous I promise we'll take it one step at a time
Discomfort you may experience, but block it from your mind
The final test, the straight line you must walk it on your own
Then rehabilitation's complete and you'll be on your way home"

We were in the room alone but I felt an overwhelming spirit
It was speaking from inside of me but I could hardly hear it
An evil voice, *Should I fear it?* I don't know it brought me calm
I could have sworn I was in the presence of my mom

Jasmyn helped me to my wheelchair, it's a new undertaking
As we exited the room it's decisions I began making
Time for new positive thoughts, a prosperous outlook
Got to be worth more than just the cover of the book
Inside I felt shook, uncertainty of what's ahead
Stay focused my new motto I started pounding in my head

11

Rehabilitation was excruciating however Jasmyn made it cool
During our stint together I found out we attend the same school
She's a nursing student working towards finishing her degree
Honestly she relit the pilot that had fizzled out of me
She really helped me to see and regain focus on what I'd lost
I'd come to college to graduate there are ways to defer the cost
Other scholarships and loans just take some time to search
Instead of tackling the journey alone see my advisors first
Many people have it worse, be thankful for my current state
I could be out on the streets or worse asleep never to wake
She argued a strong case as we debated back and forth
I began to feel something in my heart, lust had run it's course
Could she really be the one? I promised I would wait
Yet our chemistry's so strong I don't want to move too late
Do you wanna go on a date? I replayed from time to time
It's a question I fear to ask but I want to make her mine
I'm sure she won't think it's just a line, yet caution to the wind
If I'm hasty, I'll never have this chance to ask again

"Good morning to you, how's my favorite guy this morning?
Sorry I'm running late, but this morning it is pouring
And with the gloom in the sky I bring a ray of sunshine
Your release will be today if you're able to walk the line
And I have all the confidence in you, but I'll hate to see you go
Yet knowing you've gotten better is all I need to know..."

"Jasmyn will you go out with me! Hmm...maybe on a date?
Our chemistry's been building for weeks, I can no longer wait
To me you're better than great and this isn't the patient talking
I'm grateful for what you've done, aiding me in walking
But this far surpasses that you've stirred emotions I haven't felt
In a very long time with the cruel faith I've been dealt
You're indeed the sunshine to my day, please don't take it away
Without you in my life my bright future may turn gray"

"I don't know what to say, I've definitely grown fond of you too
I thought you'd never ask, of course I'll go out with you.
But for now you have a test, take some time to prepare
I'll return shortly I have to go get your wheelchair."

As she left my heart smiled, things had turned around
Shortly thereafter *was that a knock?*, I know I heard a sound

Indeed it was, as my door came open my heart ceased to beat
There *she* was standing in front of me, getting ready to speak
I tried to fight back my emotions, is it happiness or pain
A single tear creased my cheek when she said my name

"Marcellous...my son... I've missed you so much
I know you have questions on why I haven't been in touch
But for now let momma look at you, boy how you've grown
Just know I've always loved you I never wanted you alone
Words don't right a wrong, whether valid or misperceived
I never wanted to cause you pain, son you must believe
By the will of the Lord I made it back to you, I want to stay
However I will not pressure you with this I'll do what you say
School you don't have to pay I've taken care of that
Sweetheart do what you must but I want you to go back
It's a world of opportunity out there, college is a stepping stone
I know you need to assimilate, here's the address to my home
And the number to my phone call me day or night
I promise I will come to you, I'll be on the next flight."

She kissed my cheek, left the room, sobbing with every step
This had to be a day dream, but I haven't waken up yet
Jasmyn reentered the room with a quizzical look of suspicion
The tension was in the air so with words she didn't mention
She helped me to the wheelchair *"Everything will be great.*
How about dinner at my place, I'll see you around eight."

With that vote of confidence and incentive who could fail.
This one just may work, only time will tell.

12

After the completion of my test I had some time to think
The vision of my mom and her words wouldn't sink
My eyes transformed from white to pink and then bloody red
My brain pressing my skull trying to jump from my head
What led her to stay away and then come back on this day?
How dare she come and go again having things her way!
I should disregard this visit and file 13 this paper
I love her she's my mom but my pain is saying hate her
Where has she's been all this time? Maybe I don't want to know
Maybe it's for the best that I just let her go...

I quickly shifted thoughts as my doctor entered to speak
"Marcellous you're progressing fine but take it easy for a week
No more than thirty minutes on your feet, daily increase your time
I took a last look at your chart and you're healing just fine.
That's a positive sign be sure to take care of your health
All your paperwork is done you can go sign out yourself."

When the doc left the room I tried to tuck all ill feelings
Of my mom and her visit there's plenty that I'm dealing
With on this day my "release back to society"
I could sense the anticipation when Jasmyn said goodbye to me
More than anything I want this to go right I've got a fresh start
A clean slate is what I feel and I may have found my heart

Battling this bout of insecurity, she's still the one I want
She brings my heart the purity, her I'll never flaunt
If I could poise myself, *my hands are sweating*, it's a major step
Maybe the anchor of my future *don't psyche yourself out yet.*

Internal conversation with myself, hand gestures to emphasize
I've been at this for ten minutes, I'm going crazy I surmise
To my surprise Jasmyn has affected me this way
Maybe just start the engine once again and go on with my day
"What did you say..." followed by a tap on the glass
Damn near jumped out my skin as my heart raced fast
It was Jasmyn outside my car door my stomach started to spin
"You've been at this for twenty-five minutes have you decided to come in?"

She finished asking with a grin, my sweating began to cease
"I hope you're hungry I've prepared a gourmet feast"
With the least of my worries gone I'm ready to enjoy the night

Honestly, I hope everything goes just right.

Took some time to encompass the sight, I can't mess this up
She may be my four leaf clover, and the resurrection of my luck
But that's such a long time off build this one day at a time
Be alert to her unhappiness and read the unsaid signs
In my mind I could play this perfectly, but reality I'm not sure
We finally reached her apartment, I was amazed when she swung the door
True essence of a college student simplicity with a sense of ease
She finally caught my attention with the jingling of her keys

*"What do you think of the place? Here let me guide the tour
It's your first day out, let me know what you can endure."*

While showing her apartment my mind's tangent began to surface
Thoughts of my mom began to fester, *I need to focus, I can't hurt this*
Yet the seed had been planted and my concentration weaned
'Til the point Jasmyn was talking and I hadn't heard a thing

"Marcellous! Are you listening? Hello are you there?"

She caught me off guard as I exhibited a placid stare
"I'm sorry Jasmyn, the pain, I think we better take our seats."
Damn a nice recovery thinking quickly on my feet.

The rest of the evening went without incident until a lingering question from the morning
I could almost sense the question as the words had her lips forming
The question came out storming, who was the woman leaving my room
An answer I didn't want to give to Jasmyn especially this soon
I felt encompassed in a tomb it was hard to restore my breath
She knew everything else about me, this was the only thing left
I looked off to the West then gazed back to her eyes
"I'd rather not get into it, but I won't tell you lies.
The woman, my mother, I haven't seen her since I was 10
She left on my birthday I thought I'd never see her again
Then today, in my room, my heart leaped through my chest
She paid for my tuition and left with one request
She asked that I finish school, make something of my life
She nearly asked for another chance if I'm reading her precise
But I'm not convinced that will suffice, I was devastated while she was gone
I barely came to grips with it a mere basket case in my home
I simply felt...all alone, I don't know if I want her back
In my life at this juncture, that's just stating a fact"

I felt the concerned look on Jasmyn's face, for a moment my heart cringed
What was she thinking, I felt uncomfortable, another bridge I may have singed

Demetrius D. Jackson

Then she spoke...

"You know she's right, you must complete this quest
You have much to offer and you haven't given your best
As for the rest, her second chance, what does your heart say?
Forgiveness is the remedy to make the pain go away."

With those words it's so simple, *Could I let go of my anger?*
Maybe this is what's been plaguing me and generating danger
All I could do is look at Jasmyn and a calmness overflew
Inside I knew she was right, but I wasn't sure what to do.

We moved to a different topic and enjoyed the rest of the night
I felt she may be the one and I believe I may be right.

13

It's three months we've been dating and I swear Jasmyn is great
We're getting together to study tonight, I can hardly wait
She's everything I've ever wanted, fantasized, even dreamed
Any day I spend without her I start to feel like a fiend
I wonder which of these rings…maybe now is not the time
I'll give us a little longer to see if I catch the sign
But for now she's all mine, I live to make her happy
Hmm…a grown man sitting up here getting sappy
Here she comes fighting through traffic, let me stash this mag
I can sense angst in her motions, who's made my baby mad
"Hey sweetheart!" I greet, we kiss, "What plagues you today?"
Distraught overtook her demeanor what was she struggling to say?
Slowly she dropped a newspaper, then slumped into her seat
Her eyes were looking distant, cold, fatigued, and weak
I've never seen her this way, I wasn't sure how to respond

"Honey look at the paper, I nearly lost my mind."

Six dead in my hometown from the caption at the top
An unconfirmed account, as I read the scenery stopped

9-point-8 meters per second it's now hit the ground
The watery substance from the eyes now red from brown
No soul behind those eyes just a cold, lonely, stare
The physical is present yet the mind ain't there.
What's happened to this girl? Rage swirling in the wind.
Hurt by so many yet continued to give in.
Blended with surroundings while masquerading the pain
Revenge a lustful feeling that was pushing towards insane
No responses to her name, no reaction to the pleas
No pity in efforts showed with 'em dropping to their knees
It's an out-of-body experience, no control of retaliation
Judge, jury, and executioner they are facing
Many of nights she's left pacing in the shower washing them off
Started innocently with Tony and then their minds were lost
A plethora of men cumming and stumbling through the door
"Get up off her Tony, it's my turn with that whore!"
She exclaimed she wanted no more, they proceeded to batter and bruise
Thought penetration was funny with bottles and garden tools
Their stench of rancid booze was making her stomach turn
The ignition of the fire in her belly began to burn
At this present she's decimating all participating rapists

Demetrius D. Jackson

Many of days she replayed this now she works like a sadist
They're surrounded and all cornered as they played their poker hand
Tony was first to get it as he grabbed his coat and ran
Yet she had a different plan arrow arched inside his back
As his body hit the concrete you could hear his skull crack
Legolas pulling from her sack as she strikes them one by one
Cupid an arched villain arrows quicker than a semi gun
Didn't relent 'til there were none in this plane we call Earth
She's dead on the inside but it's the Black Widow's birth

Stunned to say the least, mortified and horrified
My calm and temper fortified for the head-on collide
"Baby it'll be alright" she said as calm as she could
"I debated on even showing you, then I decided that I should
I know Tony was your friend I can't imagine the hurt you feel
But I'm here to do whatever I can, baby I'll help you heal."
It all just seemed surreal and how the Joneses must be coping
I wish I could be there but that's just wishful hoping
I have no funds to fly and I might not hold it together
More than simply friends we'd be family forever
The least I could do is call, but it doesn't seem to be enough
In a closed room, a cold gust, it'll definitely be rough
Jasmyn gestured, a hug given, then my pupils began to leak
Physically I felt weak, a boxer knocked out on his feet
Uncontrollable I began to weep Jasmyn uttered, *"Baby I know.*
Let's grab our belongings it's now time for us to go."

48

14

Only a month has elapsed since Tony was taken away
And as faith would have it, it's my twenty-third birthday
My concentration in class deteriorating, my grades also slip
My mind is all over the map, I need to get a grip
Chemistry I decided to skip, told Jasmyn I'm on my way home
I need some time to reflect, to think, I need some time alone
Opened the door to my apartment a fragrance is in the air
Slow music traveling to my ears, rose petals on each stair
Quizzically I proceed, *What could this mean?* The bedroom door is parted
Honestly I'm still a little shocked on how it started:

I open the door she's on the bed purring like a kitten
With the hunger in her eyes I knew there'd be no quittin'
And I knew what she'd be getting an orgasm nothing less
Rose petals covered her vagina and the nipples on her breast
As I undressed took a deep breath looks like we're going a couple of rounds
As the music set the mood I was entranced by the sound
I decided I'd go down but first we delved into a kiss
When oddly enough momentarily I felt my testicles lift
As I pondered *What is this?* I felt a warm sensation
No doubt someone had engaged in oral penetration
A stunned look of contemplation must've spread over my face
'Til Jasmyn assured me everything was safe
It was a two-on-one affair and the stranger was no slouch
She proceeded like a pro while massaging on my pouch
I guess nothing was left out as Jasmyn slid into position
I was quick to remove the rose petals and jumped into the licking
As lust and love combined the energy was immense
I shot one through her esophagus she was working so intense
But there was no resting on the fence the girl kept on going
A little bite-tug on Jasmyn's skin had my girlfriend moaning
When I was hard again, she released me, slowly rubbed my head
Jasmyn nearly ripped through the sheets, clawing on the bed
Repositioned myself to my knees, I'm 'bout to give it to my girl
No doubt, I have to admit right now, the best present in the world
As I laid into her the female licked, Jasmyn hollered for her savior
But I think it's for the best we leave him from this erotic behavior
But then truthfully he couldn't save her, she didn't want to be saved
This wasn't forced upon her, this was something she gave
The harder I pressed, the more she received, and pushed back in return
The heat we generated in the room had my retina 'bout to burn

Demetrius D. Jackson

Then she exclaimed, *"Honey my turn!"* and pushed me on my back
Got on top and rode it 'til the conclusion of this act
The girl was off on the side, fingering, eyeing me as she did
Rocking her hips back and forth while working on her grid
I could feel Jasmyn's climax coming as she leaned to catch her spot
And obviously so was the other girl as she bellowed out, *"Don't Stop!"*
She was beautiful while on top as we rounded third for home
A trio of orgasms and just like that…it's gone

The girl, a friend of Jasmyn's, went to the bathroom for a shower
As me and Jasmyn held each other, *my devilish little flower*
Fifteen minutes later the girl reappeared fully dressed with bag in hand
Looked me in the eye and stated, *"You're a lucky man"*
Threw the bag over her shoulder and walked out of the room
It's sad but I wondered if she had to leave so soon.
But Jasmyn broke that thought, *"Don't be getting any ideas sir*
I put this together as a birthday surprise and I had to beg her
This is a one-time thing with me, a fantasy fulfilled for you
I know it's something men dream of so I made the dream come true
But I also wanted it out of your system if we're to progress to something more
Understand that I love you and I have a lot more in store."

Jasmyn was right, a dream come true and some worries washed away
We laid in bed the rest of the night and I relived the joyous day

I wake up an hour before class *last night was exhilarating*
Jasmyn's the best, no debating, saying I enjoyed it is understating
What other woman would do this for you, not many I'm speculating
She's even beautiful while she sleeps, there's no rush for her to awaken
But when she does I'll express my gratitude, let her know how much it meant
And how surprised I am at the great extent in which she went
I think she knows me better than I know myself, she knows just what to do
To comfort me when I'm down and the words to say to get me through
The unrelenting love, that pushes beyond the flesh
The more I look into it, the closer I am to ending my quest

For now I'll prepare for school… Damn it! I forgot
Art History mid-term today the proverbial rock and hard spot
These dang on well-rounded classes are a thorn in the ass
Another piece of shit I don't care about that I need to pass
Haven't paid attention well enough to go in there and wing it
Poised to be an engineer, a problem to solve, go ahead and bring it
I've got a fool-proof plan they'll never be the wiser
A code I'll script on my notebook, I'll build it like McGuyver
We're only doing name to significance and the period of the time
Abbreviate each entity, nine letters max per line

50

I'll use the notebook to write on, sit in the middle of the room
That way I'll ensure the TA's eyes can't focus in so soon
And even if they suspect something it'll be hell trying to prove
The decoding wouldn't be a simple matter, yeah I'm just that smooth
I guess I better start preparing it's about fifty of them cats
This method is fairly flawless I better keep this under wraps

I could feel my soul smirk as the last line I began to script
It was a hundred percent go and my conscience wasn't split
See it was something I didn't get, how all these other fuckers were cheats
How the curve had beat me down but those grades I had to keep
See deep inside the knowledge I gained especially major classes
And if you pit me against ninety percent I bet I'd kick their asses
So for now a pat on the back I'm intrigued to pull this off
Internal bout of competition, this will not be a loss

When I enter the classroom I scope the scene and then head to my seat
Just in time to get my hands on the test-taking sheet
I didn't hesitate a bit, yeah I cheated from the start
And while my neighboring peers struggled I was feeling smart
Not because I had an understanding but because I beat the system
Sure I could get caught, *It's only credit hours*, I'll risk 'em
But for that I worry no more eighteen minutes in and I'm done
Time to bounce out this joint and go and have some fun.

It's imperative I take a moment to reflect on where I'm at
We haven't spoken in a while I wanna clear the air with facts
For a while you turned your back, that's my perception of the situation
When I would feel the pain inside I questioned the purpose for your hesitation
I needed to heal but I wasn't patient, thus my anxiety and anger rose
I felt you weren't doing enough so we left from friends and turned into foes
But sincerely who am I kidding, it was my back I turned to you
Instead of praying, I went head strong, convinced I knew what to do
But I didn't, thus my pride and stubbornness drove a wedge through our relationship
I could never quite form the grip on the subtleness I needed to get
Every day is not going to be sunny but you must find the ray of light in every cloud
Through all of my trials and tribulations I assure you, I understand that now
Hindsight is what it is, thus I seek a futureless past
I've learned what I must, I don't want the hard times to last
I see my glass half full because I have so much to learn
I'm done trying to face this alone, dear Lord, it's now your turn

My brief conversation with the Lord, I felt a sense of ease
A new outlook on life, ready to achieve
But before I complete my mission I had some fences to mend
I've held onto this anger long enough it's time to bring it to an end

Demetrius D. Jackson

I'm not sure what I'll say, from the heart will suffice
She's the reason that I'm here the true extension of my life
I'll make the call when I arrive at home, for now I'm carefree
Graduation's approaching fast the tunnel's ending light I now see.

15

Mom we need to talk it's about the pain I feel inside
The animosity I can't hide but I feel I'm going to collide
With my ten-year-old self and the man I am today
How then I wanted you to stay, but now I wish you'd go away
I know it's an evil thing to say but you left and never returned
The longer you stayed away the faster our relationship burned
And my anger began to churn 'til it was nothingness that I felt
After dad passed away, I cursed the cards I was dealt
I almost noose-fashioned a belt, but I didn't have the skills
I figured someone my age shouldn't endure the emptiness I feel
See I went on, I progressed, the Joneses welcomed me in
Even with the hatred that I felt I thought of you now and again
But truly I'm supposed to forgive that's what I'm supposed to do

"Marcellous baby ,who are you talking to?"

"Nobody honey, just practicing my presentation in the mirror
There's a few wrinkles that I'm ironing out trying to make clearer"

I still need to make this call I've put it off for weeks
I'm not sure once she answers I'll be able to speak
But there's no time like the present, it shouldn't be this hard
Maybe it's because for years I've been emotionally scared
Now I plan to make amends forgive all transgressions
Take heed to my blessings show I have learned some lessons
I need to break this monotony, go ahead pick up the phone
Dial those ten digits and see if my mom is home
And just pray nothing goes wrong that's all that I can hope
Reach into my pocket and pull out the handwritten note.

"Hello" she says with the faintest voice, I ponder hanging up
"Hello.." she says again, *"...could you please speak up"*

"Mom it's me Marcellous, do you have some moments to spare?"
A gasp was followed by silence as if I wasn't there
Then she responded, *"Of course I do, Marcellous what a pleasant surprise"*
Just to hear her speak my name brought tears to my eyes
All my rehearsal didn't prepare me for this, *why am I so weak?*
I've gotta hold it together so she can't tell when I speak

"I called because next month I'll be graduating from school
And I wanted to invite you if your schedule isn't full
At some point we need to talk, there's things I'd like to discuss

But for now I'd prefer not to make it a big fuss."

"Marcellous, son I'll be there, I'm so grateful that you called
For a while I thought our rekindlement had permanently stalled..."

And with that it was settled I began to mend the fence
Sure it won't be easy I'm expecting things to be tense
Yet I can't rinse my hands of my anger, focus, clear my mind
I'll do what I can to rebuild our relationship this time.

Things are finally and unexpectedly working in my favor
However it's a rollercoaster ride so this feeling I will savor
Just think not to long ago my life was upside down
With Jasmyn's kindness and help I've turned my life around
Funny how it sounds, boy saved by meeting girl
Shortly after meeting she's the center of his world
Sometimes reality's a movie, make that a miniseries
You have to constantly stay in tune so you don't lose that, that's my theory
But enough with all this pondering only three more weeks of class
Then I can tell undergrad to pucker up and kiss my ass

16

The culmination of countless hours, hard work and sacrifice
Nothing else would suffice now the foundation of my life
Attention to detail and precise moving forward next phase
As the entrance music plays, I stride remembering the days
And the ways in which I progressed from a young lad to a man
From my pre-junior high wreck to being able to take a stand
On my own two feet, shoulders square, head high
To setting goals for myself that reach beyond the sky
Get to the core with what not why, that took some time to learn
That looking into someone's eyes you'll see how bright their fire burns
That there's truth in every element, even if only a partial one
And the truth is there's absolutely nothing new under the sun
That focus is your best friend and the lack of it is your worst
That it's impossible to help someone, if you can't help yourself first
That a thirst that isn't quenched is a train wreck on the horizon
That sometimes it's not about the win but just a matter of surviving
You must keep striving to do for you because it's you in the mirror
That "everything happens…" no need to spout a river

Just thoughts running through my cranium on this joyous graduation event
But it's crazy how fast all the time has really went
I take some time to observe the crowd for faces I recognize
I see my baby Jasmyn with tears forming in her eyes
As I rise for the college deans I see Mr. and Mrs. Jones
No doubt a stressful time I can tell she's being strong
But no sign of my mother, I began to think it was a mistake
I've done all I can, I reached out for pete's-sake
There I go again thinking the worse, there's a lot of patrons here
I'm just going to stay calm and keep my thoughts clear

The time has come for the speaker to address the graduating class
And just like everyone else he promised to make it fast
I'm not sure how much longer I can last, I didn't get much sleep
And my desire to hear this man talk is at best very weak
Then I peek off in the corner, speechless is putting it mild
It's as if she knew I spotted her because she lit up with a smile
It was my mom she was there she helped complete my day
I'm glad to see everything is going to go my way

It's only one more thing left to close this chapter of my life
I'm poised to accept this moment I've definitely paid the price
Finally my time has come, the words I've waited to hear

Demetrius D. Jackson

"Marcellous Thompson Bachelors of Science Computer Engineer"

PROFESSIONAL

17

Being pissed is putting it mildly, it's a nice spin put on my thoughts
The countless hours studying and the Sandmen that I fought
Hook, line and sinker it was bought, the fallacy of the American Dream
Being a college graduate hasn't afforded me a damn thing
My ire is getting steamed from career fairs to applications
"We're currently not hiring..." the constant situation that I'm facing
See it's got me back to pacing, my degree is what's in demand
But the president's economy is fucked, stealing options from my hand
I'm an overeducated individual to be employed on one end
On the other, underqualified they require five years of experience in
A vicious perpetual no-win 'cause dammit I'm stuck in the middle
"We'll keep your resume in our system" Yeah I read right through that riddle
I'm foaming a little spittle because my bills are being stacked
Collectors calling harassing but I ain't got no scratch
Yet they want to argue forth and back in the middle the line is cut
Just a new college graduate that's down on his luck

This continued on for weeks until a mutual friend had a suggestion
"I know a friend that's a manager, he'll be willing to help is what I'm guessing."
So the wheels were set in motion had to alter the resume quick
Take out the technical jargon, objective, and mentions of the internship
To be honest it made me sick, but some cash flow is what I needed
Thirty grand less than expected, damn right my ego was heated
Better than zero so I couldn't beat it, but it was still pennies I'd be paid
This wasn't on my radar, my time table goals have definitely swayed

I need this time to reevaluate, mastermind a new plan
Steps for moving forward and for when the shit hits the fan
I'll do the best I can but the job search must continue
It's gonna be a bumpy ride don't let doubt and despair creep into you
Always expect the best but...prepare for the worst
It's time to toe the straight line and put yourself first
Just another episode in my curse, but I'm not gonna fight this battle alone
I refuse to give in easily and drop like a stone.

A little pep talk to myself for a journey I care not to embark
I'll surely get the job, but it'll be a month before I start
The pressure continues to build as I work towards self-endearment
Settling for a mediocre job is far from self-fulfillment
Training is the balance of two months the plan's to be gone before it ends
Maybe a permanent position will present itself, but things don't always go as we
intend.

18

I've been at this for four months and the mess I've had to endure
My life energy is sucked out of me each time I walk through that door
I don't wanna take no more, but a job alludes me in my field
No doubt I could perform the duties, but to these employers I'm under skilled
So I'm stuck but refuse to give up this isn't the vision that I see
When I look at the man in the mirror and he quizzically looks back at me
It's an unspoken understanding we have that we're really in this together
Through sunny skies, rain clouds and tornado types of weather
I log off my headphone leash that chains me to my desk
To take my scheduled fifteen-minute break to recoup and catch my breath
I take a seat like I have nothing left as another gentleman takes a seat
I don't think I recognize him as he begins to speak

"You're Marcellous right?... I'm Sean. We were in the same class.
Analyzing Algorithms, the summer before last
I thought I recognized you, I just finished training last week
As an engineer this wasn't the job I wanted to seek
But after graduation and no prospects coming through
I ended up right here, I'm guessing just like you"

Its stunning, but it's true to say the least it's unbelievable
Two graduates with the same misfortune is quite inconceivable

"Yeah you're right, I've been here four months and still searching in vain
I bet every engineering firm in the state knows my name
But to them it's kind of a game, this is my livelihood on the line
And these so-called career fairs are a huge waste of time"

"Yours and for mine, it's like a show they're forced to do
Nine times out of ten they have their prospect and they're not gonna hire you
And this didn't come out of the blue, they've used the same excuse for a year and a half
It's gotten to the point they start to speak I think kiss my ass."
"Sometimes I wish they'd feel the wrath, have the shoe on the other foot
Let them get a glimpse from the outside and see how foul it looks
Cause for now my experience comes from books and time I take to teach myself
Hours after I've left this place, I don't do it for my health
I've tried to keep my time here stealth, clock in, then out, then home
I don't want to engage in extra-curricular activities I just want to be left alone"

"Seems like we're vibing to the same song let me complete my 'sentence' then leave
'Cause I'm quick to let them have it, I wear my emotions on my sleeve!"

Demetrius D. Jackson

We continued our conversation ten minutes over our break
And would have kept at it if my manger didn't come to tell me I was late
Unlikely encounter indeed, however a friend I may have gained
I could feel life stir back into me, what twenty-five minutes has begun to change.

19

February 14, Valentine's Day, and a plan's been brewing in my head
Led Jasmyn to believe I forgot about it, now she wants me dead
It's been weeks in the works, do something special for my baby
My lady, just maybe, this masterpiece will save me
The execution must be flawless, I had to pull many strings
Just an opportunity to show her how much she really means

6:01 is on the clock she exits the door leaving from work
Blue scrubs covers her bottom and a plain white T-shirt
She gets to her car and notices the note "Put it on I'll see you at eight
The package on your bed, I promise I won't be late."
The warm feeling that touches her heart places a smile on her face
Now I've gotta go get ready and ensure I keep pace

As the clock on the corner tolls, I knock to let her know I'm there
When she opens the door I had the right to stare
She was stunning there's absolutely no better way to state it
I'd put this vision of her up against any work of art that's been painted
Definitely pleased with the attire I purchase and the accessories she selected
The entire theme for me tonight is to let her know she's not neglected.

I take her by the hand, so soft, and lead her to the car
I help her to her seat, her eyes shinning like a star
Everything's going well thus far as 112 serenades our ears
The air is cool and crisp while the sky's forecast is clear
We arrive at our destination, reservation confirmed, private room for two
The electric anticipation grew, Jasmyn all smiles not sure what to do
We were seated by the maitre d' then the violinist began to play
"Marcellous I truly love you." Is what she had to say
On cue the waiter approached two dozen long stem roses with baby's breath
The pre-selected meal cooked by the chef and everyone but the violinist left
For my love, nothing but the best and tonight I put on the full court press
She wanted something memorable and I catered to that request
But dinner was just the coming attractions, it was time to move on to the feature
Analyzing others do it wrong was indeed my greatest teacher
As we drove across town I let her believe the night was ending
When in reality, it was only just beginning
She couldn't believe the private room and blown away by the entertainment
To see the joy it brought her was worth the savings account payment
As we pulled up to my apartment all the lights were off yet a persistent glow
Curiosity overtook her indeed she was starving to know

Demetrius D. Jackson

Again I help her from her seat, through the front door, to my room
Where the candlelight shadows dance off the wall and the mix of slow music
continues to loom
Rose petals cover every inch of the bed from bottom to the top
While the massaging oils were warming properly, didn't want them to get too
hot
Her momentary look of shock was followed by her dress falling to the floor
Her hugging me, then kissing me, then her closing the bedroom door.

20

It's the fifteenth day of May and the job situation's gotten worse
The lack of pay has drained my savings and my rent was due on the first
A drastic move needs to be made or tonight I'm crashing on the street
I need a major miracle to help me land back on my feet
The bills stacking are not cheap, and the pressure's pushing on my brain
It's real life that I'm living but yet I've gotta play this game
It's a shame I have to go through this my animosity seeks the source
Screaming bloody murder until my inner voice is hoarse
Of course I have to keep my focus, creative problem solving is what I need
It's not going to be easy but with positive thought I shall achieve

This personal talk I had to believe while my gas tank was approaching 'E'
As fate would let it be I only had two dollars next to me
But when I stopped what did I see, "Payday Advanced Loans"
A spark lit up my head but my soul began to groan
They're like sharks, I know it's wrong, but what options do I have
By the end of the day I'll feel the apartment's eviction wrath
And that's the last thing that I need thus I proceed to make that move
At this point I'm desperate and I have everything to lose

As my shadow cast upon the door I feel the bubbling in my stomach's pit
The lengths to which I'd go…this is as real as it gets
Grabbing the handle brought me fits as I was buzzed in from the inside
My embarrassment I had to subside while swallowing my pride

"If you're here to get a loan we need two forms of ID
Three recent check stubs and a phone bill would be key
A copy of your checking statement with nonstarter checks to match
Provide us with three references in case it's you we have to track
Fill out this application and be sure to sign and date
Then we'll calculate what you're eligible for, be patient while you wait."

Damn how tedious could this be, "I only have two forms of ID
The rest of those items I don't carry around with me"

"Well you can fill out the application but those items you must retrieve
I suggest you hurry up it's an hour before I leave!"

Slowly I was getting steamed at her tone and the hoops
That I'm forced to jump through if you want to know the truth
But at that point my hands were tied so she had the upper hand
Yeah I may be down on my luck but I'm still a fucking man
I gathered myself and ran to grab the items on request

Demetrius D. Jackson

I really need this money so I'll be on my behavior's best

"Here are the items that you requested, I'll be sitting over here."

"I'm sorry hun, but this banking statement isn't clear
All the amounts didn't print out for insufficient fee's you were charged
Just pick up a statement from the bank, it shouldn't be that hard!"

"It's a ten dollar fee they charge for them jokers to grant that wish
And I ain't got that type of money it's my ass you both can kiss
If you're considering I'm high risk I can let them tell you the fee
But me paying them for a statement, that will never be!"

"That information has to be in print we won't except it any other way
I suggest you scurry along it's almost the end of my day!"

Rage was replacing patience as my vindictive conscience rose
Go ahead and do what you must I'll deal with the low blows
I made my way to the bank and requested a summary about checking accounts
A pamphlet if you will that disclosed all fee amounts
With the information in hand I bounced back to "Payday" to try again
Had she had an atoms apple it'd be the battle of two men

"Aw looks who's back, five minutes 'til our closing
I hope you have my information or it's this opportunity that you're hosing
Okay what exactly is this!? I told you it's a statement that I need."

"No actually you said you need something with the printed fees
Look this is all the information you need, I've played your little game
Now go ahead and grant me my loan and don't misspell my name!"

In five minutes my process was done and I left with cash in hand
My vindictive insides were plotting for this treachery I wouldn't stand

21

That was the fastest two weeks of my life, time to repay my loan
Grateful I was able to get it, but I haven't forgotten how they did me wrong
I'm vindictive to the bone time to suffer on my account
I've already calculated how to pay 'em back in the exact amount
It'll be a hell of time to count, yeah I read the fine print
It has to be paid back in U.S. currency the amount in which was lent
They'll have no leg to stand on and vent or I walk back out with my loot
A legal loophole to kick 'em in the mouth with my boot

The plan really simple: pennies, nickels, dimes, and quarters
And 67 dollar bills, the teller laughed filling my order
Unwrapped all of the wrapped coins into my plastic Pepsi bottle
That stood two feet tall, it was the "piggy" bank model
No money counter to count the coins, they'd have to count 'em all by hand
Mix all the coins together indeed a brilliant plan

Arrive at my destination, the familiar sound from the buzzer door
Ahh the joy I'll experience to never hear that sound no more
Unsure set in her eyes as she saw the return payment
At this juncture her hands were tied and indeed she began to hate it

"Can't you go to a coin counter and just bring back all the bills?"

"Nope this is U.S. currency and I'm sticking to our deal!
I'll be back tomorrow for my belongings and my official receipt
The customer's always right is the attitude you need to keep!"

VINDICATED!

22

My professional status is on life support, I try to keep my wits about myself
As I sit alone in the bare four walled room I contemplate collecting wealth
Yet no solution presents itself but I've gotta figure something soon
The devil's in my conscience cheering on my impeding doom
I think it's a humorous thought, and then that thought avalanches
The seed has been planted now my brain is spouting branches
I've never lacked creativity maybe I'll put that to some use
Maybe a good idea but not sure where to start is the truth
I've had a flare for writing suspense thriller mysteries
I can script one and get it published and the rest is history
I can take a couple of months to prepare my manuscript
Conjure up an outline to make sure it all fits
Marcellous this is it! Time to put this plan in action
Let my pen create some smoke and script 'til it's satisfaction

Alas a plan is in the works and my confidence is building
It's been a constant rollercoaster and my relationship has been reeling
It's a lot of things in which I'm dealing with and I can sense the unsaid strain
Jasmyn tries to be supportive but she just can't feel my pain
Yes I love her all the same but now it's solitude that I seek
To focus on my writing I want to finish in ten weeks
It's the future that I'm working towards, I'm building it for us
I'm about to lean on the bond we share, I'm just asking for her trust.

23

It took a little longer than expected, three full months to complete my task
Five hours writing every day the thoughts spilling out so fast
I could feel my body trying to crash while trying to make it through this ordeal
But I was finally done writing and my spine shot a chill
It kind of felt surreal I had wrote an entire book
Now it's time to send it to the publishers and let them get a look
I'm hoping beyond hope, that all of this goes well
And that someone else is interested in the story I have to tell
It's time to drop this in the mail and it's a game of waiting now
It's the first time in some months I felt comfortable flashing a smile

With my book on the way to the publishers Jasmyn's number one on my mind
I want us to spend some time unequivocally she's my sunshine
I stop to pick up a bouquet and excitedly make my way
I'm ready to see my baby and toast this glorious day
But I'm not sure what to say I just want to hold her close
Of all the external factors I cut from my life, I really miss her the most
I finally make it to her apartment and rap upon the door
Of all the things I prepared for I didn't know this was in store.

"Marcellous come on in, please take a seat on the couch
We really need to talk our relationship is going south
I've tried to reach out to you, and you've cut me off at each turn
I know you were going through trials, but it's now my heart that burns
Do you remember when you were in the hospital recovering from your wound
The way I took care of you I didn't know I'd fall for you so soon
I love you with all my heart but you're making it impossible to progress
I think we need some time apart, I know it's for the best."

"Jasmyn...no. Please! Why are you saying this?
I know we've had rough patches, but our relationships at risk!?
This decision needs more consideration, let's take time to talk this out."

"Marcellous there's nothing to discuss now can you please leave my house"

Heartbroken and damn near speechless I entered a trance-like zone
My heart stopped beating four times as I proceeded to leave her home
I felt so alone, I forced Jasmyn to act so rash
I had someone good now I've lost her in a flash
I could hear Jasmyn sobbing from outside I know it's tearing her apart
While I believed I was doing the right thing, I was just breaking her heart
Why can't I seem to get it right? Maybe it's best we part now

Demetrius D. Jackson

She has so much going for her, I'd hate to bring her down
The truth is I now feel empty, hollow to the core
Rotten on the inside, what am I living for
Honestly I'm not sure, *if it doesn't kill it brings strength*
The cliché plaguing my mind but I'm not sure what it all meant.

24

It's a letter from the publisher three weeks after submission
After the conversation with Jasmyn I've been in no condition
To hold a convo with anybody I've been a virtual recluse
Hopefully the news in this letter will fill a void and give a boost
It's kind of loose with little weight, *what could this possibly mean?*
Probably another form of rejections I've already lost the woman of my dreams
Open it up and it would seem I'm right, *"Thanks for your submission but we regret..."*
The letter didn't affect me I was already as numb as I could get
"What the fuck is this shit?!" a tear runs down my cheek
The pain is so deep, but it's sanity I must keep
A helpless feeling overtook me I held my face in my hands
I've done all I could and exhausted all contingency plans
From my frustration thoughts ran, I need to express these feelings
A poem could really help me address this pain in which I'm dealing
I search for the pen and pad and let the pain run through my veins
I've held this in long enough, time to release the reins:

Lost Love

Lord give me a moment in creativity to express feeling from love lost
The depths of my soul is crying I can't afford this cost
From the day that our eyes met, for every word she ever spoke
Butterflies played havoc inside, but I was willing to cope
She's everything I've ever hoped, wished, dreamed that I could have
Yet it was a fairy tale I was living because we now journey on separate paths
I'm living through the wrath that hurt can bring, when you love some-
one so deep
Yet I always have the memories so I rush myself to sleep
There's a spot in my heart I'll keep for the woman who changed my life
Maybe if it's meant to be, in the future she'll be my wife.

Work of Art

A setting sun, eclipsing moon, snowy ground, a shining star
A work of art, a masterpiece, a crowning jewel that's what you are
Skillfully sculptured one of a kind, never duplicated
Unappreciated talents and mental capacity underrated
Smile kind of deceiving if you get caught in how it looks
Search the soul, look into those eyes, and you'll read the entire book

Hard times have made you appreciative and still you persevere
You're a strong, impressive, intelligent woman, you have nothing to fear
Why a work of art? Is it the beauty you possess
Making a grown successful, married man put his wedding vows to the test
Why a masterpiece? Are you perfect in every way
The way you hold a conversation and not a negative thing to say
Why a crowning jewel? Are you a princess without a prince
Guaranteed if you were searching that without would be past tense
You are what true love is looking for, you are the symbolic white dove
You open up heaven's doors, you're the Angel from above.

From that moment I began to script some verses about the curses in my past
How they harassed me since my youth and looks like they're gonna last
All the pain I've tucked away came pouring from my pen
I could hardly believe how much I was carrying within
The more I wrote my soul would grin because the light I began to shed
In those instances the world's weight was off, I laid embedded issue down in the bed
More images rushed to my head I spent three hours writing nonstop
I paused, grabbed a meal, then wrote 'til one o'clock
When I laid me down to sleep I felt the fog clear from my mind
An inner voice kept repeating not to ignore the given sign
I wasn't quite sure at that moment but my tunnel was condensing
An external force would be the catalyst that did all the convincing.

25

The clouds are parting slowly while the sun rays shine brand new
As I head off to lunch I read the verses that came through
What an unbelievable high I'm not even phased by work today
I can't wait to get back to writing and get this day out of the way
I notice Sean, I grab a seat and exchange my "hello" with his *"hi"*

"You seem to be on cloud nine and I bet I know the reason why
You and Jasmyn got back together, I'm assuming a make up
Hopefully you can keep it strong if you're having any luck."

"Jasmyn and I still haven't spoken however I let my pen stroke some words
For some reason I couldn't stop it was hinging on absurd
It was a riveting experience the way the words massaged the page
The creativity I felt was fueled by my inner burning rage
I reached a stage of desired calm and drifted off a happy man
I can't wait to get home tonight and do it all again."

"Damn Marcellous that is awesome, you should let me read one or two
I'll read them between calls and at the end of the day return 'em to you."

"Sure…why not…in fact take the entire pad
Let me know if it's really good or if I'm a raving lunatic gone mad."

Sean made his way back to the call floor while I scarfed my remaining meal
I'm sure to get Sean's honest opinion he always keeps it real
I could feel another surge on the horizon, I needed to focus on separate thoughts
Categorize 'em, set 'em aside and give a title to each one caught

I fought myself the rest of the day I couldn't concentrate at all
This poetry writing was getting the best of me I disconnected every other call
My conscience didn't waiver at all as I took the headset from my ears
"Damn! That isch is tight!" is all that I could hear
Sean met me at my desk and slammed the tablet on the table

"That was some deep introspect shit you pulled out from the stable
Marcellous I kid you not you need to work on a publishing deal
The expression in your words is something people will feel."

"I tried with a publisher once with a story that I wrote
They basically sent me a denial like a stowaway on a boat."

"Who said you need them at all, do that isch all own your own
All you need is your creativity, an Internet connection, and a phone
The rest is time and research, and formulating a plan

Demetrius D. Jackson

If anyone can do this I have all the faith you can
'Cause Marcellous you're the man when you put your intelligence to use
Here's the opportunity you've been waiting for, give yourself a boost
The sky is your only roof, but shoot pass that to a star
Everything happens for a reason, think what you've gone through thus far
It's all lead you to this moment, and finally awakened your gift
You were destined to make this happen, an opportunity you can't miss."

What Sean was saying...is he right!? Is this what my soul was talking about
Is this the path I'm meant to take, am I supposed to follow this route
I'm trying to make sense of this, I'm nowhere near where I should be
Professionally I've been screwed, it's time to invest in me
The more I let it sink into my psyche the more sense it began to make
The CEO of my own company, a step I'm willing to take

"Sean I think you're right I need to put some more thought in this endeavor
I have to give it to you, this thought is pretty clever."

We parted ways I left from work with more than poetry on my palette
Sean gave me plenty to think about and all of it was valid
To start a publishing company is an undertaking I have no clue where to begin
But I have to structure is right and let my voice be heard in the end.

26

Two weeks in I'm two feet deep in the middle of building a foundation
The mere thought is exhilarating it has my blood racing
Now I'm chasing the American Dream as elusive as it seems
I'll force this dream to come true, nothing can stop it, not a thing
First step the company name and the registration with the state
It'll be "Mirage Productions" and we're not going to be second rate
Next up I want a logo, I'll hire an artist to put it together
I'll give them the thought in my head with the hope they'll make it better
Then it'll be the ISBN and information about work copy written
I see the vision clear in my head and pieces are finally fitting
Now a harder decision to be made, printing binding and distribution
No doubt this will be the highest hurdle that's no illusion
While perusing on the Internet a few binding companies came to light
I need samples of their work before deciding the winner of this fight
At night I continued writing after I retired from the day at work
Basically working two jobs, from which only one pays, the pressure hurts
But it was worth the agony, if in the end, I'd be excused from the rat race
I'd control my salvation then I would set the pace
Yet the distribution is what kept haunting me, how to get it in the hands
Of people all around the country if I planned to have any fans
And have them cheering in the stands for a performance I gave live
I need to figure this out if the dream is to survive

The more I thought about it I realized there was more I needed to do
A business plan was in the works but I needed marketing too
Staying true I knew who I could call who has experience in this field
Having them agree to help me would be a huge ordeal
But I feel that I can trust them so I had to make the call
A marketing plan was needed and it was time to roll the ball

Before the phone started ringing I hung up and rethought my stance
It's been a while since we've talked, I need to get my mind out my pants
I dialed the number again, it rang, *remember why you called.*

"Hello" I tried to speak but for some reason my voice stalled
After a moment I was able to muster, "May I speak to Sasha if she's at home."

"Sasha! It's for you! Pick up the phone!"

By now she's all grown a recent graduate with a marketing degree

"Hello"

Demetrius D. Jackson

"Sasha, it's Marcellous. Long time no see."

"Marcellous wow! A voice from the past. How are everything these days?"

It's sad I'm thinking about the sex we had in many different ways
"Sasha things are going well, look I called to ask you a favor
I'm going to make you an offer hopefully you can sink your teeth in and savor
I'm starting my publishing company in which at best my marketing's weak
I thought we'd use this opportunity to help each other get on our feet
I know marketing isn't cheap and I don't have much money to provide
But I do have a plan that will help us both to stride
All the materials I'll cover cost for, but I can't pay you for your service
But I do have a plan so please don't get nervous
Ten percent of all profits gained for the first year the book's in print
Then I'll hire you for all other marketing needs, Five years, a fair price you'll get
Just let me know if you're down with it and I can give you more details
I'll be putting the success of work in your hands, it's your job to help it sell"

*"Well Marcellous indeed a proposition given, how on earth could I say no
I'm ready whenever you are to tell me everything I need to know"*

From that point we spent three hours on the phone discussing what I'd need
I felt comfortable after the conversation ended a positive choice I believe
The harder I worked, the clearer the picture became, but plenty's on the plate
I'd have the foundation built in no time if I keep at this current rate
But for now I needed a break that I would spend all alone
Jasmyn stayed on my mind but I wouldn't call her on the phone.

27

Saturday, a beautiful day, I'm prone to rest and relaxation
I'm off from my job today and thoughts of business brings hesitation
I've been going at this nonstop since my conversation with Sean
Writing is sixty percent complete and I'm still right on time
On the office side of things a printer and binder has been secured
Distribution in two spots if only one agrees I'll endure
Was that a knock on the door? Not many visitors these days
I guess I alienate most because currently I'm stuck in my ways
Yet I snap out of my daze and proceed down the stairs
Open up the door I could hardly believe who was there

"Well don't look so dumbfounded are you gonna invite me in?"

Sasha asked with authority and trailed it with a grin
"Sure where are my manners?" as I greeted her with a hug
"Please take your shoes off I just cleaned this rug"

"I know I should have called first but I had to see the surprise on your face
You have every right to be mad I just hope that's not the case
I could have played it safe but where was the fun in that
Then again you may have said no and that's just a fact
Anyway the reason I'm here, I have samples to help advertise
I wanted your personal opinion to see if they were appealing to your eyes."

What Sasha came up with was magnificent I was pleased beyond belief
One more check to add to the checklist and this was a big relief
We discussed the rollout strategy, that would be key to success
Timing was our top priority to ensure visibility was the best
We took a moment to rest, which spelled doom from the start
Sasha began to nibble on my ear the erotic key to my heart
She was smart to remember this spot from sessions in her room
Next thing I knew we were kissing, it was all happening to soon
She lead my hand to her breast and slid her tongue through my teeth
She initiated tongue wrestling and it was awakening a beast
I couldn't cease thinking about Jasmyn so I slowly pulled away
While Sasha tugged on my bottom lip I prepared myself to say
What I knew was true deep in my soul that Jasmyn's my true love
I've gotta give us another chance it became clear from above
How the "everything that happens..." happened to us in our separation for a while
It finally became clear to me and I had to crack a smile
The pain I felt through our breakup forced me down the path of poetry

Demetrius D. Jackson

My true calling's gift to the world was always there inside of me
I now know how to proceed and give her what she truly desires
It's time I find my baby and fully light the flickering fires

"Sasha indeed I'm flattered and a tad bit intrigued
But honestly crossing these lines is the last thing we need
No doubt you are astonishing, blessed with impeccable beauty
Doubly nice you can work your brain, not an airhead cutie"

"But Marcellous I've longed for you since our last sexual encounter
You didn't mention a Misses so I assumed you haven't found her
With the offer you put on the counter I figured we could make a perfect couple
Especially with the belief there'd be no feathers that I'd ruffle."

"The assumption you've made isn't accurate me and my girl are on a break
Jeopardizing our future together is not a risk I'm willing to take."

"But we make such beautiful music while our bodies harmonize
Just once we'll cross the line, feed your curiosities rise
Let the amazement and surprise of me showing up here today
End with us satisfied and both having it our way
I could tell when you kissed me back the desire you felt for me
My ignitions ready to be started, you just have to insert the key"

Truthfully I could see the loophole and Sasha was seeing it too
If I acted on these emotions would it be a day I'd live to rue
In a quandary on what to do 'til I rationalized it wasn't wrong
No need for a disturbance so I proceeded to unplug the phone

It was silence in my home we made room on the couch
There was no turning back she placed my finger in her mouth
She locked me in her eyes as she slowly licked the tip
I felt entranced in her spell as I slowly fell into her grip
She removed her shirt and her bra with her nipples already erect
Then fed me her left breast 'til I ingested all that I could get
I proceeded as if an infant, Sasha gasped under her breath
Slid her hand down her panties and her fingers never came to rest
'Til she decided to remove them slowly and stood up on the cushion
I was faced with her vagina so my tongue got to pushing
And her juices got to gushing as she leaned forward to take more
When obviously she had her fill she dropped to the couch on all four
Prefaced she's not a whore but she yearned anal penetration
Like the kind you see on video or the erotic station
So I lined up for the task and after we cleared the initial insertion
We uped the tempo a little and got our bodies working
Grabbed some hair and got to jerking she was salivating every minute
No need to pull it out she wanted me to cum all in it

Took her suggestion and ran with it, it was an unexplainable feeling
Sat back kind of amazed then Sasha sent my head reeling
Because Sasha wasn't done dealing she laid my appendage on her tongue
Engulfed it fully then I knew it'd be more than one
Indeed she worked it well and made my neck hairs stand
Tugged at her nipples with her left and massaged my balls with her right hand
I have to hold on as long as I can but I could sense me getting weak
I unloaded from the repository onto the inner part of her cheek
She didn't let it dribble or even leak as she released me to get some air
She moved across from me and sat in a chair.

I thanked Sasha for the session but advised on keeping a professional focus
In the face of this awkward moment, deep inside I really hope this
Doesn't ruin our working together because within she has a gift
But we'll bring it to a halt if it puts Jasmyn and I at risk
We exchanged a handshake, a hug, a kiss I watched her drive down the street
I still had the urge to call Jasmyn and tell her we needed to speak.

28

A week had passed since Sasha's visit and it was emptiness that I felt
Jasmyn was on my mind it was something I couldn't help
Constant struggles I fought daily on if I should call or let her be
The truth is…I really wanted her back with me
It's her smile I'm dying to see, mentally a plan I formulated
Once devised I wouldn't debate it, my power of words are underrated
I know now she's kind of gated, unsure about letting me close
I have to get her to understand it's her that I need the most
Nonetheless I need to make the call the time is never or now
I dial the seven digits and wait on the ringing sound.

After a few moments on the phone we agreed to meet at Jasmyn's place
I'm pouring my heart on her carpet no need to play this safe
I gathered everything that I needed this my be my final chance with her
An old familiar feeling, the butterflies began to stir
Arriving at her place was all a blur as I mentally prepared
The things I longed to share to reinforce that I cared
She was standing there, a masterpiece, in the door frame
Motioning for me to hurry and get out of the pouring rain
Which made me recall it's the same, weather from when I first asked her out
Maybe things are coming full circle, that's what I'm talking about
The words came stumbling out my mouth I had to compose myself to speak
Literally I heard the echo around the room each time my heart would beat

"Jasmyn many things have changed since the last time that we spoke
The hurt really cut deep but I found a way to cope
And to be honest it truly steered my life now I'm traveling the correct street
Which actually brings me to the reason I insist that we meet
There's something I need to share with you please listen close
By the end you'll understand why I cherish this the most.

Will You...

I don't know where I should start, or even if I have the right
I think about you constantly and I'm miserable at night
Somehow I lost sight that our hearts were intertwined
I removed mine from the equation and left you on a lifeline
Then had the nerve to ignore the sign as your heart withered away
There's no healing words that I can say but I truly regret the day
That I put myself in solitude and left you all alone
At the time I thought I was doing the right thing, but hindsight proves
I'm wrong
I've been shown the error of my ways and the path I need to follow
I want to make it up to you, each moment of your sorrow
If we could just borrow from when we first met and move forward from
that time
I know we're destined to be together and everything will be just fine
It'd be a crime to let you go so I'm dropping to one knee
Jasmyn I truly love you, will you marry me?

The tears streamed down her cheekbone with adornment in her eyes
As I pulled the ring from my pocket to intensify the surprise
While on one knee I grabbed her hand as a tear hit my wrist
Looked up in her eyes I knew she couldn't believe this
It felt like forever before she answered as all time stood still
Still unsure of her reply, and when she answered I felt a chill
A "*yes*" was shrieked so high that a nearby glass cracked
I placed the band on her finger and gently pushed it back
Hopped to my feet to give her a hug and I swear everything just felt so right
This is the women I'll come home to each and every night
My heart was soaring like a kite to be back in the arms of my baby
For any present I've ever received, this is the best one she's every gave me
We were engaged just like that I was feeling completeness in my life
Mirage Productions neared its debut and Jasmyn would be my wife
Just a few loose ends to tie up and I'd see the balance of my work
Knowing I've defined direction for my life is the biggest perk.

29

A few questions still need answers in which I need to take a serious look
I'm about ninety percent complete but I still need an ending for the book
And the distributors have me shook because they're wavering on a quicksand surface
The release is in five months and they're making me a little nervous
I'm seriously playing a timing game with not much buffer in between
If the schedule falls behind it will ruin everything
Too close to realizing this dream time to apply the full court press
It's the fourth quarter now exert until no energy is left

First things first, I have to settle this distribution
If I don't get this settled there will be no horns tooting
I'll call my contact with the company to find the reason for the delay
I swear they'll need to give me an answer by the end of the day
There's no way I'll let 'em get the best of me, I'm keeping my foot pressed to their throat
Until they look at me with starving eyes like I'm their last breath's hope
I'll note, jot and script so they don't pass me around
It's time to start this final act and see how it goes down.

"Brian this is Marcellous CEO of Mirage Productions
You've been teetering on a response for months I need to know something
I feel my kindness is being trampled it's a simple yes or no
I came to you exclusively but there's other places I can go
In case you didn't know there's others chomping at the bit
Please pardon my French but I'm getting sick of this shit
Matter of fact I lunch at noon you have 'til then to present a reply
If I haven't heard a thing then to your company I say bye-bye
And in three months you'll wonder why you let this mega opportunity slip
While you're sitting at home unemployed from the new one your boss had to rip."

I feel I played my cards right let's just hope he takes the bait
I've placed all my eggs in this basket let's just hope it's not a mistake
But just in case I need to identify, a contingency that will work
I sense despair trying to creep in, tugging at my shirt
I'm a problem solving genius, self proclaimed anyway
Credibility is what I need and I know just how to make that play
There's some other phone calls I need to make, I'll make it the last resort
Multiple distribution spots I'm bound to not come up short

As I go to pick up the phone it rings while in my hand

"Marcellous Thompson please." I don't recognize the voice of this man

"This is he," I keep it bland, "what's the nature of this call"

"This is Jerry, Brian's boss, I hope I'm not bothering you at all
I'd like to apologize for the delay, Brian's been out on short-term leave
And he has a massive client list, something I could hardly believe
We've had a review over your work and everyone agrees it would seem
We'd like to extend an offer and welcome you to our team
My secretary's drawing up the papers and then legal will review
Once we have their blessing we'll send it out to you
In the meantime if you have any questions be sure to call me direct
I think we'll do fine together in business something I'm sure we wont regret."

I confirmed my fax number we said our good-byes, what a turn of events
A quick sigh of relief I'm no longer feeling tense
Maybe his boss got my message or maybe Brian passed it along
Regardless of the reason I had a distributor once off the phone
I almost broke out in song even though I can't hold a tune
I'm almost at that star I think I'm hovering by the moon
Soon everything would be complete I have my writing to finish up
Then I'd send it to my editor and if I'm having any luck
I'd have it in the hands of the printers less than five weeks from now
I'd have to see the contract sent to see how my marketing will go down
Posters, counter displays, bookmarks and window hangs
And before you know it, everyone will know Marcellous' name
But I still need to concentrate keep focus on the final task
Patience is the key no need in moving along too fast.

Conclusion

I worked feverishly the last four months one of which was to complete the book
Sealed up the distribution and received the first official printed copy to take a look
Worked well with Sasha, after the incident at my place, marketing was a smash
The book's been on the market for a week, damn it went so fast
From interviews, to book signings, and tonight's first week numbers release party
And I'm still out here talking to you, I'm about to be tardy
But truly I don't mind at all it's been interesting reliving those events
They've all molded me to who I am today, though some were dicey and tense
But I wouldn't trade it for the world because without 'em I wouldn't be here
I've overcome a lot and I've conquered all my fears
It's just one thing left to do, witness the numbers when they arrive
Then go join the party with my fiancé by my side
Ah...the sweet sound of the fax, the anticipation has come to an end
I must say thanks to all who've purchased this book, the first week numbers are in...

Shadow World
Productions

Shadow World Productions Proudly Present

TURMOIL

Through Insurmountable Circumstances…
She is Vindicated

Written by
Demetrius D. Jackson

Turn the page for a preview

Demetrius D. Jackson

Intro

I'm secure within myself and I feel I shall not fear
Yet my inner voice is yelling about the clues I need to hear
I sense my right eye tear as I look at the empty proof
I want to ask the question yet I cower from the truth
He keeps me under a roof, not just me but also my son
A condomless wrapper's not enough so to my lawyers I dare not run
I'm not trying to bring this about but I can't ignore the signs I see
We intertwined our hearts for eternity he wouldn't cheat on me...would he?

1

"Sir I'm not sure this charge is correct, I haven't been to a hotel
I'm sure if you pull the receipt it'll have a story to tell."

"Mrs. Thompson you're correct, it's not your John Hancock on the line
But the signature of your authorized user and I can read it just fine
It reads Lamar Thompson and I'm assuming it's your spouse
Maybe if you search you'll find the receipt in your house."

"Thank you for your time." I feel my suspicions coming true
My stomach's feeling knotted and I'm not sure what I should do
How on Earth could this have happened, his hotel charge on my card
The truth is it doesn't matter because now our marriage has been scared
And he's worked really hard to keep this secret out of sight
And if he takes another trip out I'm gonna follow him tonight
Yet I fell this isn't right, look at the level to which I've stooped
But I refuse to be contained like a chicken that is cooped
If he's cheating I need to know and confront him is a must
My baby Marcellous is home I hear the tires from the bus
For the time being I need to concentrate and show some affection to my child
I need to get my heart under control because it's pounding really loud

"Hi mom I'm home from school, we went on a field trip to the zoo
We saw lions, tigers, and bears oh and a large giraffe too
Who had a clue owls who'd and that bats could see in the dark
We were in the under water aquarium and I almost touched a shark
Of course it was through the glass but mama I wasn't scared
Then we watched the apes and the bananas that they shared
It was such a great experience I can't wait to do it again
I still have a report to write could you please pass me a pen?"

That's mama's baby boy, he's so smart and energetic
"Marcellous mama loves you I never want you to forget it."
He's the center of my world and for him I want the best
For him I'd give anything even my last breath
For now my soul wont rest even though my heart has slowed
The audacity he has to be a cheater I admit is really bold
Revenge is really cold and if it's true I wont relent
I've given my heart and soul where has all the honesty went?

I hear the bumbling fool, fumbling with his key
I have to play it cool but I'd like for his groin to meet my knee
The discovery I can't let him see, this night has to be the same

Demetrius D. Jackson

He opens up the door and addresses me by name

"Kim honey I'm home, hmm something smells divine
Seems like dinner's ready and I made it just in time
And where's that son of mine? 'Hey Marcellous where you at?'"

"He had a paper to write so he's sitting out back
Here let me hang up your coat and be sure to wash your hands for dinner
And it just may be your last one you damn ungrateful sinner..."

"What was that baby?"

"Ah nothing just thinking about the day
Speaking of which, how was yours anyway?"

"Still got my nose to the grind and I have to go back to work
I didn't want to miss dinner and I needed nourishment for the spurt."

"Do you have to go back tonight, I was hoping for time alone..."

The conversation was interrupted with the ringing of his phone

"...no I'm at home are you sure this can't wait?
I understand. I'll be there a quarter after eight
Baby I'm sorry, I have to go in earlier than I thought
We have to do a review of the new software we just bought
It's got me caught in a bind 'cause I'd prefer to be here with you
But my boss is demanding and I have to do what I have to do."

"Baby what can I say, I know your job demands so much
Should I stay up late and wait or go ahead and pack your lunch?"

"Kim I'm truly sorry but it'll probably be a late night
If the sandman comes calling go ahead and throw the fight."

He's walked right into the trap and my stomach's feeling queasy
His mistress had the nerve to call and it makes me feel uneasy
But I have to follow through I have to execute this plan
My nervousness is evident with the shaking of my hand.
Yet I refuse to let this man win thus this issue I must press
Composure is a must and I'm gonna do my best.

"Leg, thigh, or breast what's your pleasure for this night?"

"A thigh and a breast will do me just right"

His response with a smirk and my feelings started to hurt
I started envisioning his corps just laying in the dirt
Break our bond for some skirt, no! it can't be justifiable
Rid these homicidal thoughts, 'cause tonight I'll see my rival

With my own eyes I must witness, I'm hoping a false accusation
But the call with the credit card company isn't erasing
From my memory it replays no matter how much I'd like to forget
Tonight the unveiling, get to the bottom of this shit.

During dinner Marcellous relayed his trip to his dad
He's only experienced happiness I'd hate to see him sad
This situation is making me mad, I don't want pain to enter my child
Trying to balance all these thoughts in my mind they start to crowd
There's a dark cloud over this house, but some light's about to be shed

"Come on Marcellous, dinner's over, it's time to prepare for bed
Your dad has to work and I'm sure he'll tuck you in
But first you have to bathe and polish up your grin..."

"Aww, mom..."

"No buts, now get on up them stairs."

"Dad always has to work late, that really isn't fair!"

As Marcellous headed up the stairs I felt the dejection in his step
And my heart felt heavy and inside my soul wept

*"Kim dinner was really good I need to grab a change of clothes
But first I think I'm going to finish off these tasty dinner rolls."*

As Lamar picked up the rolls and followed our sons path
I felt the moment coming closer and the fury of my wrath
Had started to bubble deep yet I still prepared for my trip
Fears' head was trying to rear but I had to get a grip

I took this time to clear the table and start the dishwasher
Put the clothes in the dryer from our fully loaded washer
Folded the clothes that still remained and put away Marcellous toys
He must be out the bath; I don't hear the splashing noise.

Lamar was tucking away Marcellous and reading him a bedtime story
He's so good with our son I'm not so sure he
Would cheat on me, but there's so many questions floating about
Five minutes into the story Marcellous was knocked out
Lamar kissed me on the cheek and headed out the house
And I followed in his foot steps quiet as a mouse.

2

It's imperative I keep my distance I don't want Lamar to spot
Me trailing close behind him cause then he's bound to stop
So far the journey we take is job ward bound, maybe he does work
But that still doesn't explain the lipstick stain I found on his shirt
Maybe I'm a jerk for distrusting my mate
But I must follow through for sanity no more excuses to make
But so far it's seems so innocent, he is pulling into his job
It could all be made up in my head then we definitely have a prob
I watch him park, get out the car, and walk up to the door
He enters, disappears, I guess I was expecting more
Looks like I have no leg to stand on, I guess I could go home
Then all of a sudden a car I recognize comes right along
It's the car for our next door neighbor, I didn't know she worked here
Wait a second, no she doesn't, now it's all becoming so clear
She walks up to the door, but you need a security badge to enter
Then Lamar comes back down the stairs and with a kiss he greets her
I nearly loss my dinner at that moment, she's married with a baby
Could he have been cheating with her this long that it's his maybe

He grabs a hand full of her bottom as she nibbles on his ear
Her nipples were getting perky because the blouse she wore was shear
Again my eyes began to tear as she went down on him in plain view
Horrified and motionless I didn't know what to do
The more I tried to move away I couldn't look away from his adultery
She took him like a pro and the scene was getting sultry
For minutes I was frozen in shock until they started their second round
The hurt was burrowing to my core it was time for me to leave now
I tried to yell but no sound, then I shifted the gear to drive
I felt my heart still pounding but I didn't feel alive

I dare not go home, I'm in too much of a fragile state
My concern is my baby's at home alone, what if he were to awake
I pulled over on the side of the road as the numbness found my limbs
The vision of them in that lustful embrace, I've given everything to him
Please remove this vision, the replay is worse than the actual sight
Revenge is the only thoughts I could conjure but I know it isn't right
Tonight he's hurt me worse than any words he's ever said
Cheating is bad enough, but he crawled into our neighbors' bed
And to think of all the outing that we have jointly held together
The way we kicked off the new years we were the trend setters
How could he let her into our bond…obviously it's now broken

Out the window with my hopin' I'm choking on the words I've spoken
The hurt is circling my enter being and stirring up unforgettable pain
The symbolic cloud has opened in reality and now it starts to rain
I hang my head in shame because maybe I'm not woman enough
It's a plausible reality I need to face although swallowing it is tough
Maybe on myself I'm being to rough, it's he I should be angry with
I'll be sure to contact my lawyer but it's revenge I must first get

For now I need to get home I have a son for whom I must care
I'll never speak with him of his fathers treachery, it's something I wont share
I hope to spare him of this embarrassment but when we separate it'll be hard
And to think I may have never found out if it wasn't for my credit card
I start the car and drift through the lanes as I start to make my way home
The question I can't seem to answer is where did it all go wrong?

I cooked, cleaned the house, and birthed his legacy in name
I loved him and adored him now I feel it's all in vain
The reality's driving me insane, if we were having problems he should have spoke
It didn't even have to be spoken words, I would have took it in a note
I'm so furious...who could be calling my cell phone at this hour
"Hello"

"Hey Kim I just hopped out of the shower
And I was thinking about your cobbler and some vanilla ice cream
I'll bring the Hershey's syrup and it'll make a great team
How about it? I'm sure Lamar is probably at work
And if you don't mind I'll probably wear my pajama bottoms and a t-shirt"

Hearing Teresa's words my feelings hurt and uncontrollably I weep
"I saw Lamar cheating on me tonight, it's a vision I'll never forget
I'm not good company right now..."

"Nonsense I'm on my way
That sneaky son of a bitch will live to rue the day
I'm coming with my tools, we're castrating his little man
And the pebbles he calls balls and then put them in his hand
Cause obviously he ain't got any or he would have told you and separated
He probably didn't want to give half, I bet that's the thought he hated
When I'm done..."

"Teresa stop! Violence isn't the key
We can talk. Meet me in ten minutes, it'll probably be therapeutic for me."

As we hung up the phone, thoughts swirled through my mind
This hurt has cut deep I have to pay him back this time!

Made in United States
North Haven, CT
04 May 2024

52101588R00055